Sweetly Sings the Donkey

Sweetly Sings

J. B. Lippincott • New York

Vera Cleaver

the Donkey

ACKNOWLEDGMENT

For her assistance in providing those research materials necessary to this work, the author wishes to express gratitude to Adele Oldenburg of the Florida Community College System.

Library of Congress Cataloging in Publication Data
Cleaver, Vera.
  Sweetly sings the donkey.

  Summary: When fourteen-year-old Lily and her family move to Florida, it falls to her to keep her family together and start a new life.
  1. Children's stories, American. [1. Family life—Fiction] I. Title.
PZ7.C57926Sw 1985   [Fic]   85-40098
ISBN 0-397-32156-2
ISBN 0-397-32157-0 (lib. bdg.)

1 2 3 4 5 6 7 8 9 10
First Edition

To my pioneers,
all of those good, funny people
who were and are my family.

And to our friend Clair Marquis Parks,
who knows the why of things.

Sweetly Sings the Donkey

One

One day Charlie Bleeker decided he was truly in love with Lily Snow. He wanted her and would have walked through a brick wall to get her. Often and often he had lain in his solitary bed thinking long thoughts of her and dreaming long dreams about her. He thought that she was the most desirable creature ever made. Charlie was sixteen. Lily was fourteen.

That evening they met by appointment, and Charlie, leading the way, said, "I wanted you to see the new barn my dad and I just built. It's his now, but someday it'll be mine. I like barns. And hay. Sometimes when everybody else has gone off like they have now, I come in here and lay down in the hay."

"I like the smell of it," murmured Lily, gazing at a pile of dried hay. She hated anything that had to do with farms, and couldn't smell a thing except

Charlie's close dampness. He had closed the doors
to the building, and in its eerie dusk his plump face
and square teeth made Lily think of a Halloween
pumpkin. The Bleekers' donkey had come up close
to the barn to roar its coarse song: "Hee-haw. Hee-
haw."

Charlie did not know how to be glib. Leaning
toward Lily, he laid a nervous, wet hand on one of
hers. His voice was brave, and in the middle of his
wheedle it cracked. "Let's lay down in the hay."

Lily drew back. "Oh, we mustn't."

"We won't do anything," gabbled Charlie. "I don't
want us to do anything. I just want us to lay down
in the hay so I can be close to you. I just want us
to talk. I want to talk about us getting married."

"Sweetheart," said Lily, and bent upon Charlie
her little-girl's smile. Her lips were moist like a
baby's. She wore a simple cotton dress and a light
sweater. The smallness of her waist brought the
tears to Charlie's heart. It was Lily's purity that so
attracted him. Through those pouting red lips of
hers nothing mean or ugly had ever passed. She was
so good, so perfect, so kind. Lily was a lady. She
couldn't help the way she walked. The way she walked
was an invitation only to him, Charlie Bleeker. To
Lily, Charlie could not, could not say the things he
had said to other girls.

Charlie wore one piece of jewelry, a ring on his

left middle finger. Its dark green stone was surrounded by pearls. Charlie had a little trouble getting it off. He reached for Lily's hand and pressed the ring into her palm. "I bought it from a guy who was hard up for cash, and didn't pay much for it. It's not worth anything, but I want you to have it."

Lily looked at the ring and raised her eyes to meet Charlie's. In a country way he was kind of sweet, but she had had enough of his whining attentions. He loved her or thought that he did, but he was the type who could love a lamppost if the post would only love him back.

"Charlie," said Lily, "I can't be your lamppost."

"What?" said Charlie. "What?"

"I can't take your ring," said Lily. "Here. Take it back. Save it to give to somebody else."

Charlie's wet eyes were brave and tragic. "No. I don't want anybody else to have it. I want you to have it. It isn't much, but don't you lose it. When you look at it, think about us."

Around the ring in her hand Lily curled her fingers. She turned and put her arms around Charlie. She allowed him to kiss her once, and it was flabby, without urgency.

Charlie let his breath out in a shuddering sigh and tottered away to the doors of the barn. He opened them, and the thickening night streamed in.

Lily walked home alone, and though the three

5

miles were nothing to her, a thought crept into her mind: It would be nice to have another fool along, but no, I don't want another fool.

Away way out, far across the state, far beyond the breadth and vision of Lily's little town, the Black Hills of South Dakota slumbered. In between, looming all around, appearing inexhaustible, running out in all careless directions lay the prairie. Some lights in the town were on, and these were contentedly dim.

In front of what her father called his grocery store, Lily paused long enough for a look in through the bare window expecting to see her father fussing over his bookkeeping or bent over one of the pieces he was forever fixing for resale. She had a clear view of the store's single, cramped room. Her father's grocer's apron hung from its familiar hook. He had given up for the day.

That's his life, thought Lily. And the lives of the rest of us. Some potatoes, some flour, some coffee, a can of this and a can of that. And junk. We are junk.

Lily's father was a junkard. He saw a fortune in the junk of others, and when he wasn't behind his grocer's counter prowled the town's alleys and vacated houses for discards: clocks, broken chairs, picture frames, a crock or some dishware that had belonged to somebody's great-aunt. A hoe without a handle was a real find. He repaired these things and installed them in a discreet corner of his store, and occasionally his salesmanship netted a sale.

Judson Snow was not a salesman, nor was he a grocer. Groceries were not in his blood. He didn't know what was. He had tried railroading and brick-laying. Once he had worked as an orderly in the state's asylum for the insane. For this job a physical examination was required. The young examining doctor had pleasantly told him that he had a heart murmur.

"Is that going to keep me from getting this job?" asked Judson.

"No," replied the doctor. "But you ought to watch it. You ought to consult your own doctor about it."

"I don't consult doctors," said Judson, and put his shirt back on. To the point of reverence his mother had believed in doctors, but he had always cured his own illnesses with a little barley soup and a day in bed. He was afraid of doctors and what they might tell him.

Judson was one of those people who should have lived back in the history-making days of South Dakota, but history had made its way without him. There was no more frontier. Wild Bill Hickok and Calamity Jane had long been dead. There were re-servation Indians, but they didn't want to fight. The stagecoach had been replaced by the automobile.

There weren't any more gold nuggets lying around in gulches. Or were there?

An old cowpoke who liked hunting for gold more than he did poking cows came into Judson's store one day and reported finding nuggets of the precious metal "as big as a woman's thumb."

Judson asked a shrewd question: "Where?"

The cowpoke's answer was just as shrewd. "In the Hills. I have been to the Black Hills and I'm going back."

Judson almost said, "Take me with you." He thought that he might like to climb on a horse and gallop off to the Hills, there to sit around a campfire with cronies, listening to them talk about the wonders they had seen, listening to himself talk about the wonders he had never seen, listening to the coyotes howl. He thought that he might like to see the return of the buffalo herds and the gold-prospecting days. He had heard some mouth-watering tales about Alaska and thought that he might like to go there. He thought many things and in weak or tired moments tried talking with his wife about them. She listened and thought many things, too. She was waiting for him to come to his senses. He thought that he already had them. He wanted out of his body but was trapped in it. He had a case of the wanderings but knew that he had to work and stay home even if home wasn't what anybody had ordered.

The Snows had seen many homes. They were experienced movers. Since they didn't own any furniture or anything else that weighed much over twenty pounds, they were deft at moving. This was not always by choice but was frequently a slippery, stealthy response to a landlord's angry demands for past-due rent.

Now, in this town the Snows called home, their home was a little different from others they had known. It was roomy, and the price of the rent included some passable furniture. Its windows were curtained, and when it was night and the floor lamp in its living room had been turned on, it almost looked like a place somebody might want to come back to.

Tonight the lamp was on. On a pallet beneath it sat five-year-old Patrick, youngest of the Snows. He was wide awake and was playing with some empty spools.

Lily said, "Hiya, sweet stuff," and sat down beside him. The house was unusually quiet.

Patrick lost interest in the spools. Glaring, he set his pansy eyes on Lily. "Feed me," he said. Those were his two favorite words.

Lily rose, went to the kitchen, and returned with a piece of cold, thick bacon. Patrick snatched it from her fingers and began sucking on it.

"Where is everybody?" asked Lily.

Patrick couldn't or wouldn't say. He rolled his

blissful eyes and worked on his bacon.

Lily crouched beside him and leaned to pass a hand over his head. His hair was pale brown and downy soft. He liked his mother, but Lily was his anchor, his lifeline. She was the one who showed him how to do things. From her he had learned how to fake a fit and scare people so they would run away. He was never embarrassed by anything Lily did or said. In some strange places and in some strange company he had spent some lively times and some quiet ones with her. He had seen her smoke a cigar and swim naked in a river. He had felt the sting of her tongue. Her laugh made him laugh.

Patrick had the light weight and the agile build of a young monkey, and was never so happy as to run around the town with Lily, whether in the rain or the sun made no difference. As an infant he had ridden on her back, papoose style. Now, when they were out on the town like that, he was attached to her with a rope, one end of it tied around her waist and one around his. When they were out on the town like that, he liked to see her flip her skirt and cut her flirty eyes at the silly men, but whenever they were together like this and she started with some of her queer talk he was bored.

Except for his bacon Patrick was bored now, for Lily was making herself comfortable on his pallet and was preparing to talk. She put her knees together, raised them, and set her chin on them. She might have had the best-looking pair of legs in all of South Dakota. "La," she said.

Patrick pulled the bacon from his mouth and looked at it. It wasn't white enough or limp enough yet. He put it back in his mouth and sucked.

Lily examined her legs. "I wish," she said, "I could think of something to invent so I could be a heroine. But we've already got the light bulb and the sewing machine. Somebody beat me to the wheel. Do you think I should tie myself to a stake so I could be another Joan of Arc?"

Patrick produced a belch.

Lily extended her hand so that Patrick could see what was in it. "That clod Charlie Bleeker. He wants to marry me, he says. He thinks I don't know that even in this jumping-off place it wouldn't be allowed because we're too young for that. You see this ring, dumpling?"

Patrick's sidelong glance acknowledged the ring in Lily's palm. It wasn't anything to eat, so he was indifferent to it. "Oh boy," he said.

"Charlie gave it to me," said Lily. "It's to loosen me up so the next time he asks me to jump into a pile of hay with him I'll do it. But you want to know something, dumpling?"

Patrick didn't want to know anything. He turned

his head and his eyes sought the door to the room where his mother and father spent their nights. It stood open. "They went out," he reported.

"La," said Lily, laughing. "What Charlie doesn't know is, if I never see him again it will be too soon. And another thing. When I get ready to jump into a hay pile with anybody who's male, I'll own it and the barn, too. It'll all be nice and legal."

"I said they went out," repeated Patrick in a loud voice. A flush came into his cheeks and spread up to his hairline. "Danny hit me," he said. "He is a bad boy."

"In a minute I'll go and hit Danny," promised Lily. She put a hand inside the neck of her dress and withdrew the chain she wore around her throat. It was one of her father's junkard relics, a throwaway piece salvaged from somebody's attic or moving-day alley pile. It was thick and dull, and from its links there dangled a gold-plated miniature football equipped with a link of its own, a mounted elk's tooth similarly equipped, and a signet ring. To these gifts Lily added Charlie's. Mentally she referred to the eager donors of these as the "Breathless Boys."

Now she restored the chain to its nesting place and rebuttoned the neckline of her dress. "The Breathless Boys," she said. "They like to give me things. They know I'm not going to give them anything back, but they don't care. They do it anyway. Why do you think that is?"

"Because they like to look at you," said Patrick, little sage that he was. "You're pretty, and the other ones are so ugly it makes them throw up."

The chain around Lily's neck wasn't resting comfortably. She gave it a little tug and it shifted and settled. "It's my getaway bank," she told Patrick. "As soon as I get enough in it I'm going to sell it, and then you won't see anything of me but my dust rolling down the road. It's going to get me as far from this place as I want to go, but from the looks of things that won't be anytime soon, so you'll have time to finish your bacon."

Patrick had finished with his bacon and threw the soggy string of it into a corner. He issued a command. "You go hit Danny."

Along with Lily, a breeze passed through the house. It was early autumn, but the Snows' part of South Dakota was not yet ready to loosen its hold on summer. The first frost had not yet come. The Snows' doors and windows were open, and in their front yard wild geraniums still stubbornly bloomed.

Lily did not bother to knock on the door to her brother's room. She pushed it open and, with a hand on a hip, stood looking in at Danny. As always she was moved to pity or curiosity or annoyance, she couldn't tell which. But as always one clear thought shone out: He lives where it's strange, and he's never going to tell the rest of us where that is.

In his pajamas Danny was sitting in the center of

his bed, just sitting there with his eyes on a wall, though it was blank. The ceiling light was on, and under its bare glow he looked too small and too delicate to be twelve. For a boy he was too clean.

Danny had a bicycle, and when he wasn't in school delivered groceries to the well-heeled matrons of the town. For this service he was sometimes given a quarter or a half-dollar. He despised the money, but more than that he despised being told that he was always to make his deliveries to the back doors, never to the front ones.

Danny never passed up a chance to let Lily know that, so far as his idea of a sister went, she was as shabby as the last rose of summer. Now he transferred his attention from the wall to her. "Where have you been?"

Lounging in the doorway, Lily lifted her hair from her neck. Danny always made her feel that she needed a bath. "I was out looking at a barn. It was red."

"Every time something happens you're gone," said Danny.

"Patrick told me you hit him," said Lily.

"He spit on me," said Danny.

"You touch him again and I'll hang your face on that wall," said Lily.

Danny was not threatened. He was far, far away, floating in some numb dream. "We got a telegram," he said.

Lily dropped her hands. "Who from?"

"Nobody we know," said Danny. "A lawyer."

At once Lily was suspicious and alerted. In the town of Presho a lawyer had tried separating the Snows from their car. In the town of Parkston another had succeeded, making it necessary for the Snows to catch trains when changing their places of residence. Was that last wily little fellow still after them? What for?

Lily stood erect. "All right, we got a telegram from a lawyer. What did he want?"

As if he had been asleep, Danny stirred. He left his bed, went across the room to his dresser, and opened its drawers. From under his bed he hauled out two pasteboard boxes and began packing them with the contents of the drawers. "Dad's half brother in Arkansas died," he said.

"That old ragpicker," said Lily. "He was enough to gag a maggot. I remember that time he came to see us. Brought us some grapes. Grapes. About ten pounds. And all we had between us and starvation was a can of flour and enough lard to make biscuits. Mama cried, she was so embarrassed, and I went out and stole a duck so she'd have something to cook. I told her an Indian gave it to me."

"You're not decent," commented Danny.

"Uncle Scott didn't even say thank you," said Lily. "He ate his part of that duck like he was at a trough."

Still at his packing, Danny said, "He left us some money."

The air was so still. When she was able, Lily asked, "How much?"

"The telegram didn't say," answered Danny. "The lawyer has been looking all over South Dakota and Wyoming for us. As soon as he gets a telegram back from us he'll tell us how much. Uncle Scott left us some property, too. It's in Florida. We're going to Florida as soon as we get the money and Papa sells his store. He and Mama have gone out now to see about getting us a car. You'd better go start getting your things ready."

It took Lily a while to take all of this in. In a daze she returned to the living room and Patrick. He had found his metal spoon and his kitchen pot and was playing drums.

"Patty," said Lily, "we're going to Florida."

Patrick gave his pot an exceptionally energetic whack. "Did you hit Danny?"

"I told him he'd better not touch you again," said Lily. She lay on Patrick's pallet, and presently she didn't hear his banging. She heard the thrill of the Atlantic Ocean as it nudged the Florida shores. Florida was warm even during winters, so everybody walked around near-naked. Oranges hung from every tree. The towns had sidewalks, and there weren't any farms.

Beyond these fancies Lily could not go. She was acquainted with some First Americans, Indians from a nearby reservation. And she had had conversations with the cowboys and farmhands who came to her father's grocery for their tobacco and flour, but none of these had ever mentioned Florida to her. She didn't know anyone from there or anyone who had been there.

To stop Patrick and his racket, Lily dragged him onto her lap and told him, "Our good uncle has died and left us a pile of money and a beautiful house to live in, so now we're going to Florida. Help me think about that, Patty. Let's just sit here and be quiet and think about that. We won't cry. Uncle wouldn't want us to cry. He hurt and didn't have anybody to take care of him, so he decided to go on. Now he's better off where he is. We're going to be better off, too, pretty soon."

It was part of Patrick's charm that he had not outgrown his ability to go to sleep anywhere. Against Lily's shoulder he slept. She carried him to the room and bed they shared. He was someone to be sheltered.

The Snows knew about shelter and the lack of it. What they didn't know about or how to handle it was a windfall, because they had never had one.

Lily's mother and father came home in a black Chevrolet. Judson Snow said that it was one of the finest automobiles ever to roll out of a car factory. For Danny and Lily he sounded its horn and displayed its other important qualities. He had parked it in the Snows' front yard. There was white moonlight.

Strutting and crowing, Judson walked around the car, wiping dust from its shine. "It's secondhand and isn't ours yet, but it will be just as quick as that lawyer who is handling things can get our money to us. Your mother and I sent him a wire, and as soon as he gets it he'll start putting things into high gear. We don't figure on that taking too long. And then guess what?"

"Florida," said Lily. "Danny told me." Her eyes felt bigger than they were. She felt bold and humble. All else forgotten, already restless for departure, she wanted to throw herself at her father and kiss him. Regarding his elation, she asked what she thought was a sensible question. "How much money did Uncle Scott leave us and how much property?"

Her father looked puzzled. He walked around the car again and came back to admit that he hadn't thought about the money or land in terms of amounts. His quick frown was for Lily and his laugh was for himself, but the laugh was not the embarrassed kind. It was tinged with a surge of freshened youth and the youthful stuff dreams are made of. "The lawyer," he said, "didn't state the amount of anything in his telegram. Telegrams cost money, don't you know that?"

"No," answered Lily, who had never sent a telegram or even been inside a telegraph office.

Her father had opened one of the car's doors and was reaching inside to search for something. He found what he looked for, slammed the car door, and, waving road maps, suggested that everyone go inside so the maps could be studied.

Delaying this, the town's sheriff came rolling down the street in his official car. He stuck his head out of its window and wanted to know what the horn blowing was all about.

Said Judson, "My wife and I were just showing our new car to our kids."

"We are going to drive it to Florida and take up residence there," said Martha Snow. A dainty little person with radiant hair, she was like Patrick—someone to be sheltered. "We just learned this afternoon that my husband's brother has died and we are the beneficiaries of his estate," she said.

"That is something I have never been," remarked the sheriff. "Nobody ever died and left me anything."

Judson was modest. "We don't know yet how much of an estate there is. Scott was only my half brother. When my dad married his mother I left home, so I never really got to know him except to find out he was the secretive sort. I don't know where he made his money. I didn't even know he had any until this afternoon."

"What are you going to do about your store?" the sheriff wanted to know.

"We're going to sell the inventory and hand the key to the building back to its owner," was the answer.

"There's a town ordinance against blowing car horns at night," informed the sheriff and drove off.

The lights in the Snows' house burned late that night. Around the oak table in the kitchen the family, all but Patrick, sat and adjusted themselves to their new condition. On the back of the stove a forgotten stew simmered its watered life away.

It was not a good experience to eat what came from Martha Snow's kettles and oven. She didn't understand the theory of yeast breads or pot roasts. Her failures were never her own. They were a large matter because Judson Snow still remembered his mother's fine cooking and frequently made some tactless comparisons. Yet he was in love with his wife and so forgave her everything. He was confident that she remained in love with him though time after time he had disappointed her. For his lack of drive, for the way he slid along with things, always dreaming of change but only dreaming of it, she had been angry with him and seriously so. But she was his girl, and the rainbow was still out there.

Martha's remark had nothing to do with her stew. Tailored to the occasion, it was one of her innocent, girlish pieces, drummed up more for her benefit than anyone else's. "Scott was a fine, Christian man," she said, "and we mustn't forget him in our prayers." She couldn't remember what the inside of a church looked like, it had been so long since she had seen one, and only prayed during a storm. She was cold-sweat-scared of lightning and thunder.

With a glint in his eyes, and holding a green crayon, Judson had the road maps spread out on the table before him and was charting a travel course. "People, this time we are going to go in style. We are going to sleep in hotels and eat in their dining rooms. We'll start out fresh each morning and drive till somebody sees something he wants to look at. Then we'll stop. Does anybody besides me want to see a mountain? There will be mountains in Tennessee. I want to stand on a mountain and throw my hat to the wind, and I'm not going to worry about it coming back."

"I only care about how we are going to live when we get to Florida," said Martha. "I don't care much about what's in between."

"I don't know what I want to see," said Lily. "Lots of water, I think. The ocean."

Judson bent to lay an arm across Danny's shoulder and to smile into his blank face. "Son, don't you want to stand on a mountain and throw your hat to the wind?"

Danny drew back. "I guess so. I hear Patrick," he said, and jumped up to fill a glass with water. Carrying it, he left the kitchen.

What lungs Patrick had. Two minutes later his enraged scream filled the house. "Lily! Danny touched me! He touched me! Lily!"

The many aches of this place, thought Lily. We will leave them here. The aches of us, she thought. We'll leave them here.

"He means we'll be sleeping in a tent and doing our cooking over a campfire," said Lily.

Her mother fell back in her chair. "No! We can't!"

"We can," declared Judson, and jumped up to pull Martha to her feet and dance her around the room. She was not to be converted to his point of view that night and spent the greater part of the next day aimlessly wandering around in the yard, digging in the black dirt. Angrily she made a pile of weeds, and refused to eat or drink what Lily took out to her.

Uneasily Lily stood looking out toward the prairie and saw nothing but its monotony. She took in a breath of wind, and another. Soon the warmth would go out of it and the snarling winds of winter would come. The winter would be white and lock them in. In deep snow she and Danny would trudge to school and back again. Water for everything would be meltwater—melted snow. The water pipes would freeze, and the clothes on the line would rattle with freeze. Surely there was a better place than this. Surely in Florida there was always plenty of pipe water. And there the wind blew in sweet from the ocean and the wild grass grew green. Wasn't it possible that in Florida even the donkey sang sweetly?

With a somber look into the future, Lily knelt to lay a hand on her mother's shoulder. "Mama, don't

Lily wrote a farewell note to Charlie Bleeker but could not force a farewell tear, so she sprinkled her notepaper with water drops and was gratified to see the inked letters run together.

It was hurry-and-wait time. Responding word from the good-news lawyer did not come and did not come, and there were days when Lily looked at all of the packed boxes stacked in the hallway and shook her head.

Her father was patient with her doubt and again displayed the frayed telegram. "No, it's no trick. Who would want to play a trick like this on us?"

"It's somebody wanting to pour cold water on our parade," said Lily.

Her father laughed. He had put his store inventory up for sale, but nobody was interested in quantity buying. Money was scarce, and in spite of its age the town hadn't grown up very much. Its bank was a one-story wooden structure that looked like something out of an old wild West movie, and when there was a mail dispatch and the postmistress was late getting to her job, the mail sacks were trustingly left in the doorway to the post office. Some of the town's people still ground their own coffee. Most of them turned up their noses at factory jellies and pickles.

Patrick was delighted with all of the attractive commotion going on at his house. His pot and his metal spoon had been taken away. He had watched them disappear into a box containing other pots and other spoons. His pallet blanket was gone, too, but there were other things. Out there where there weren't any houses or people, out there where the wind shook the grass, there were the furry little puppies. Prairie dogs, Lily called them, and they came up out of their holes to roll in the sun. They tumbled over each other and chased one another. They barked. To hear the grass talk, Patrick leaned toward it and cupped his ear.

Tied to his rope and tied to Lily so that he couldn't dart away, Patrick trotted around the town, and every once in a while grinned and shrieked a gleeful command to a shocked face. "Hit him! He's a bad boy!"

Patrick laughed to see the shock on the faces. He loved that and loved going to Papa's store. Today in Papa's store he ate dried prunes and dropped their pits into the barrel where the pickles were

instead of throwing them onto the floor as he usua. did. For today was different. Papa's eyes said s They knew a secret and they were naughty in th way the eyes of a grown-up are when trying to make something right of something that is a little wrong. Papa had a fistful of papers and held them against his cheek.

"You've heard from the lawyer," said Lily.

"Yes," said her father. "Take Patrick and go home and tell your mother."

"The puppies," said Patrick. "I want to go see the puppies." His want was denied, and he howled on the way home and threw pebbles at Lily. She gave his hands a sharp slap, and he said, "I don't like you." But during the evening meal he sat on her lap and gave gentle attention to a small scab on her chin.

There was much talk.

"It is not settled yet," said Judson, "but the lawyer is anxious to get it that way, so it won't be long." He had a pad and pencil and, with a spark in his smile, made his first notation and whipped out his secret. "People, there isn't going to be as much money as we thought there would be, so we are going to Florida the pioneer way."

Martha swallowed the last bite of her apple fritter. "The pioneer way. What does that mean, Jud?"

With a dramatic flourish, and with Lily leaning to watch, Judson made a sketch on his pad.

think about how it will be getting there. Think of how it will be when we get there."

"You don't understand," said her mother. "There is no house in Florida waiting for us. All your uncle Scott left us was raw land."

Lily sat back. Under her high-necked shirt the chain around her neck suddenly felt too tight, too short. When it came, her voice groped for its weak words. "I thought there would be a house. Nobody said so, but that's what I thought."

Her mother pulled another weed and savagely tossed it aside. "No. No house until your father puts one up for us. That's what he intends to do. Until then we will camp on raw land and sleep in a tent. In sleeping bags. Knowing your father, can you imagine what kind of house he will put up for us? Can you, Lily?"

There was no answer to that question. None was expected, but before she left the yard and went back to her puttering in the house, Lily was backed into giving a promise.

With dirt on her face and a tremor in her voice, her mother said, "We will go. We must because there is nothing for us here. We have found that out." Knowingly then she exacted the promise. "But that means you too, Lily. You are not to leave us." She was faced with something she could not beat, and so was Lily.

So Lily gave her promise. "I won't leave you, Mama." And held her temper back. Babies, she thought. Mama and Papa are a pair of babies, worse than Patrick. Neither of them is ever going to grow up. Now we are going to pioneer it all the way to Florida, and when we get there Papa will slam a few boards together and say, "Here's your house." And Mama will sit out under a tree and sulk. If I had a lick of sense I'd get hold of that Breathless Boy, that old one who couldn't wait to give me his elk's tooth, and tell him, "Look here. I've changed my mind. If you still want to run off with me and if we can find somebody willing to marry us, let's go." That old boy would do it. He's crazy about me. But la, he would want to take his old-maid sister with us. He can't even scratch himself without first asking her if he itches. And pretty soon she would want us to come back here so we could live on her farm. I would have to get up every morning at four o'clock and go down and slop the hogs. I guess I've got more than a lick of sense.

Lily took herself and her sense back into the house and gave one of the boxes in the hallway a vicious kick, putting a hole in its pasteboard side.

On departure day Patrick's metal play spoon fell from the hole, and he grabbed it. "My spoon!" he cried, and darted out to watch the last-minute preparations.

For a hauling trailer Judson had plunked out some of the Snows' cash, and had been obliged to throw in most of his grocery inventory, his accumulation of junk pieces, and Danny's bicycle. Into the trailer went a canvas tent, five sleeping bags, apple crates doubling as food boxes, duffel bags and a basket filled with clothing, some tools, some blankets, sheets and pillows, two camp stools, a few books, an assortment of eating and cooking utensils, a satchel of medical remedies, a box of catchall, two water pails, and the balance of the grocery inventory. Covering all of this was a tarpaulin with corner fasteners. It was time to go, and for the last time Martha stood in the back doorway of the rented house looking out toward the prairie. A dawn haze lay on the land. There was no green or blue in it.

Under Martha's outer clothing, securely fastened around her waist, was a money belt containing the Snows' entire cash capital. Not an astounding amount, its total was a little scary but was more than she and Judson had ever before had all at one time. She had to believe that it would be enough, and turned to walk back, to lay the key to the house on the oak table. This time she and her family weren't running. The rent had been paid and the car was theirs.

Traveling east and south, the Snows left South Dakota that day and entered the corn country of Iowa. From their road they saw grain fields and farmsteads. In the fields there were new haystacks, and from time to time hordes of birds blackened the sky. Riding the air currents, they flew in loose formation, wheeled, and hungrily descended. They knew the bounty of those fields.

Sitting between Lily and Danny in the back seat of the car, Patrick ate animal crackers, and climbed over Lily to stick his head out of the window in the way of a joy-riding dog. He was ordered to pull it back in, and he howled. He wanted to stop and smell the sunflowers. He wanted and wanted and was scolded and scolded. He slept and when he woke stood in the seat to trade stares with Danny. Sullenly Danny stared him down and withdrew to his corner.

"People who live in Florida don't have to wear any clothes unless they want to," commented Lily. "It's so nice and warm down there all the time."

Danny gnawed his fingernails and stared out the window, counting trees and bushes.

"Cotton grows in Missouri," said Lily. "Did you know that?"

"I don't care what it does," said Danny, and closed his eyes, while in the front seat of the car Martha and Judson talked, fell silent, and talked again.

Patrick could not be still, and Lily produced a piece of foresight, the family comb and a square of waxed paper. When covered with the paper the comb became a musical instrument, an extension of voice and breath. Lily set her lips to it and played tunes for Patrick.

Lunch was a roadside affair of grocery bread spread with canned meat and water from the thermos jug. In midafternoon the temperature might have stood at seventy degrees, and the thermos jug was empty. Judson said he had had enough of driving for one day and turned onto a secondary road, drove into a meadow, and turned again to park the Chevrolet in the protection of some red cedars. He had a nose for fresh water. "I smell it," he said, and bounded off to come loping back full of triumph and plans. "I found it and it's clear. Tastes good. There might be some fish in it. If there is, we'll have trout for our supper. I'll be the cook."

"We are going to spend the night here?" said Martha.

"That's the idea," answered Judson. He began spouting directions. "Lily, take Patrick for a walk. Martha, will you dig out my fishing tackle? Wait, I'll have to get the tent out first, but before I can do that I'll have to unload some of this other stuff. Danny boy, you and I will get our hotel set up and then we'll go try our luck with the fish. Martha, where do we want our kitchen? Which way is the wind coming from?"

Doubtfully and a little fearfully Martha looked around. All of her kitchens had been rooms with stoves and faucet water. Because she was afraid of snakes she was afraid of sleeping in a tent. She could not put her heart into this pioneering of Judson's and gave him a short answer. "Put the kitchen wherever you think is best, Jud. I'll help you. I think the wind is from the north. I forgot to pack your fishing tackle. I remember now that I forgot and left it."

Judson's frown came and went. He was riding on a high wave, and the adventuring of it was his glory. "Well," he said, "so much for the fish. For our supper we'll have eggs. I brought some nice fresh brown ones." Good-naturedly he began to unload the trailer, to hand down sleeping bags, boxes of foodstuffs, and boxes containing eating and cooking ware.

Danny received the tools needed for setting up the tent. He looked at them and looked at Lily.

"The heavy thing with the claw on its end is a hammer," she said, and laughed at her brother. He was so ignorant of boy things. He was such a kid, so tragic, so finicky, so afraid he might get a little dirt on his hands or some on his clothes. He had never known the joy of mud puddles or that of an alley fight. Danny was joyless.

Lily took Patrick by the hand and led him away from the trailer and the car. They went through red and purple grasses, and Patrick got down on all fours to observe some traveling caterpillars. "Fur worms," he said because he was Patrick and could invent names for things.

He and Lily located the moderate stream that coursed through the meadow, cupped their palms to drink from it, and sat on its rocky bank to give the water time to settle in their stomachs. In front of them stretched stubbled fields and beyond them there was a house.

Patrick had an idea. "Let's go see that house."

"Let's not," said Lily.

Exploring their bones, Patrick set his hands on his knees, and after a moment of this had a one-word comment: "Eggs."

"Don't think about them," said Lily.

"Why do we have to eat them for our supper?" asked Patrick.

"Fate," answered Lily.

"What's that?" said Patrick.

"You'll find out," said Lily. "Go find some more fur worms, but don't go near the water. Stay where I can see you." She sat on a rock and watched Patrick trot off. Sundown was still hours away. The sky was empty and the air smelled of some far-off something, some child something that was done with and gone. Lily couldn't remember what it was. I want to go home, she thought. But where is that?

She stood and looked out to where Patrick, still absorbed in the mysteries of his fur worms, wandered after them. He had his head down and paid no attention to the man coming across the fields. The man came abreast of him, checked his stride for an instant, and came on.

Lily returned to her rock. When the distance between her and her visitor had shortened, she saw that he was maybe twenty-five or thirty. His waistline said that he had made too many trips to the midnight refrigerator. It overlapped his high-pocketed trousers. Its bulge spread upward and stuck out. "How do," he said.

"Oh," said Lily, "I'm all right."

Said High Pockets, "I was on the other side of the creek when you and your folks pulled in. I saw you."

"We're camping," said Lily.

High Pockets pulled a blade of grass and ate it. "That's a mighty cute little boy you got out there."

"His name is Patrick," said Lily.

"Heh," said High Pockets. "That must be Irish." He bent and with his sleeve cuff tried to remove a purple stain from the toe of one of his shoes. "Blueberry," he explained. "About an hour ago when I was taking my pies out of the oven, one of them got in the way of the turkey and spilled over. On pie day I always roast me a turkey, too." His scrubbing was not improving the stain and he gave up on it. "You ought to know," he said, "that you're on my property."

"We didn't know we were trespassing," said Lily. "Do you want us to leave? If you do, we'll go as soon as Patrick gets tired of chasing caterpillars."

"It's not as if I liked spoiling things for people," reasoned High Pockets. "Little children least of all."

"Patrick will understand," said Lily. "He is not a usual child. He is used to disappointments."

"That man back there putting up the tent," said High Pockets. "Is that Patrick's dad?"

"That's my father," answered Lily.

"I thought he might be your husband," said High Pockets.

Lily began to have some idle fun. "I am a widow."

"You look mighty young to be that," said High Pockets.

"The women in my family don't show their age," said Lily.

High Pockets moved to seat himself on the rock vacated by Patrick. "I live here all by myself. I have never been married."

"You probably haven't met Miss Right yet," sympathized Lily. "When you do, you won't be able to get her to the courthouse or the church fast enough."

High Pockets pulled another blade of grass and ate it. "It must be hard on somebody who looks like you to lose her husband."

"It was very hard at first," said Lily. "But I'm over it now and can enjoy life again."

"I enjoy my life," said High Pockets.

"You've got a nice place to do it in," said Lily.

Some thought dribbled into High Pockets' common face. "It will be all right if you and your folks want to camp on my property tonight so long as you watch your fire and don't leave me any mess to clean up."

"You are kind," murmured Lily. "We won't make any mess and we will watch our fire."

On his rock, High Pockets shifted his weight. He wanted more talk and leaned forward confidingly. "Like you say, this is a nice place for me to enjoy life in. I wish everybody could have it as good as I've got it."

"You should see the places where Patrick and I have lived," said Lily. "The last one was like a prison. We had to crawl over the landlady's bed to get to the front door."

"But a man gets lonely," said High Pockets.

"We all get lonely," said Lily.

High Pockets continued to lean. "What did your husband die from?"

"It was a rare disease," answered Lily. "I can't pronounce the name of it. Its victims have fits."

"I'm healthy," asserted High Pockets. "So was my dad up till a few days before he passed on. It was a green potato that killed him. Then my mama went, too, so now I'm here all by myself. I've got a few hired hands, but today they're not here. They've all gone off to the rodeo. I told them I was going to dock their pay if they did, but they went anyway. They've all got women, and tomorrow they'll come dragging back here all calf-eyed. None of them will be worth shooting for a week."

"Probably they're young," observed Lily, "and only looking for a little fun and some comfort."

"Heh," said High Pockets. "Most women don't think about giving comfort. All they think about is getting it. They want to get married."

"I will never marry again," said Lily.

High Pockets eyed Lily. "I like women, but I don't want to get married. Right now I know six or seven women wanting to marry me, but I don't want to marry any of them. They wear lipstick and put perfume in their hair. Perfume and lipstick is a waste of a man's money. My mama never wore either one. She was a hummer. They don't make them like her anymore. She kept the house and saw to it our bellies was never empty. She drove the tractor as good as my dad, and there was never the day she wasn't right out there with him doing her part. I never saw her look at herself in a mirror."

Probably by the time she got through with all of that she wouldn't have recognized herself if she had, thought Lily.

"She made all of our soap, and when she wanted

37

her hair to smell good that's what she did it with," declared High Pockets. "She'd wash her hair with it. She had a recipe for it and I've got it now. I make all of my own soap. There's nothing smells any better than a bar of good, plain, homemade soap, and it don't cost near as much as what you buy in a store."

With a hand Lily shaded her eyes and watched Patrick. He had gone up onto a little knoll and was crawling around in the grass, so all she could see was his back sticking up.

High Pockets was preparing to go. Standing, he was looking back toward the Snows' campsite. There was yet no wisp of smoke to say that a camp kitchen had been established. Said High Pockets, "Every so often gypsies or somebody like that come through here wanting to camp on my property. I don't let them. I tell them to move on, but you folks are different. Right away I saw you were different."

"We are that, all right," said Lily.

"Camping people always need to wash something," said High Pockets. "I've got a batch of my soap in my storeroom now, and if you wanted to go back to my house with me I'll give you a few bars."

Lily accepted this generosity. Patrick wasn't sure it was generosity. Following High Pockets and Lily across the fields to the farmhouse, he lagged behind, so that Lily had to go back for him. In a fierce whisper he told her, "I don't like that man. He belongs where it's dark."

"He belongs where he is," said Lily. "He's a farmer and this is a farm."

"I've seen other ones that look like him," insisted Patrick. "They don't like little kids. They only like girls like you. You better be careful."

"There's nothing to be careful of," said Lily. "We're just going to that house up there to get some free soap. That man is going to give us some, and the walk will be good for us. When we get to his house, you can keep your big eyes open and your ears, too, but for right now shut your trap and come on."

Patrick said that when he got to High Pockets' house he was going to keep his big eyes and ears open. Under his breath he muttered threats.

Across the fields the wind blew dry, and across the fields went High Pockets, Lily, and Patrick. High Pockets had a strong, methodical step and only from time to time turned his head to glance at Lily. He talked in spurts. "I feel like I've been knowing you a long time."

"Sometimes it happens that way," said Lily.

"Some people you can know all your life and you still don't know them," said High Pockets.

Lily agreed. Up close, High Pockets' house looked like him in that vague way that dogs sometimes look like their owners. It was big. It was plain. It was simple with a touch of prudery. Its yard was grassy. Along fence rows there was tall goldenrod.

High Pockets said that Patrick could play in the

yard while he and Lily went inside to get the soap. Patrick stuck his jaw out and said he didn't want to play in the yard.

High Pockets' tongue came out of his mouth to moisten his lips. The expression on his face strained for cheer and patience. "Heh," he said. "Of course you don't. I was forgetting my manners when I said that. Instead, how would you like to see my kitchen?"

"What's in it?" asked Patrick.

High Pockets described what was in his kitchen— blueberry pie and a whole, stuffed turkey just out of the oven. "I'm a good cook," he said. "How would you like to try some of my cooking?"

Patrick was making greedy noises. "How much of it can I try?"

"I don't ever put limits on what my visitors eat," said High Pockets. "You want the whole turkey, you eat the whole turkey. You want a whole pie, you eat a whole pie. If your stomach won't hold it all, you can take what you want with you when you go."

Patrick allowed High Pockets to show him the way to the kitchen.

In the hall, Lily waited. It was gloomy and, except for a coatrack with a man's jacket slung over its top, was bare. There were closed doors along its length, and after several more minutes of waiting Lily walked to one and turned its knob. It swung open, and curiously she entered High Pockets' storeroom. Unquestionably it was the room in which he dried his soap. Most of the floor was covered with wide strips of butcher's paper, and on these lay thick white oblongs of what was unmistakably soap. To Lily's touch they were firm and dry. She walked around them to reach the room's only piece of furniture, an easy chair with an attached footrest sticking out on hinges.

Lily sat in it and felt its broken springs dig into her. She listened to the heavy footsteps in the hallway. It was High Pockets returning from the kitchen. She could hear him opening and closing doors along the way. When he came to the storeroom, he pushed its door open and tried to close it behind him. It wouldn't stay closed, but he seemed not to notice. He was annoyed and in a hurry but was pretending to be neither.

"I found your soap," said Lily.

Taking care not to step on any of the soap bars or the paper, High Pockets skirted around the room to stand in front of the chair. "That chair is not comfortable. That's why I put it in here. I don't ever sit in it."

"I think it's very comfortable," said Lily.

"There's room in it for both of us," suggested High Pockets. His face said: I am a man. He picked up his feet and made them move him around to the side of the chair. He crouched beside it and in a

fretful voice said, "I haven't ever been in love before."

The man is a simpleton, thought Lily, and drew
herself to the far side of the chair. This was a mistake, for immediately High Pockets was in it with
her. Adjusting his weight, trying to make it fit, he
threw his arms out and tried to pull Lily to him,
but his weight, his fatness, was in the way, so that
he succeeded only in forcing her shoulders and head
to incline toward him. In a gusty whisper he said,
"Come closer. Can't you come no closer?"

"No," answered Lily. High Pockets had a hold on
her neck. She met his eyes. "Are you trying to stran-
gle me? Let go. There isn't enough room in this
chair for both of us."

High Pockets released his hold on her. "Then let's
get ourselves out of it and go somewhere else," he
wheezed. He heaved himself up and out and headed
for the door. When he reached it, he poked his head
out but then hastily drew it back in, pushed the
door closed, and took several backward steps.

Out of the chair, Lily said, "What is it? What's
the matter?"

"The little boy," exclaimed High Pockets. "He's
out there and is acting like there's something wrong
with him."

"Let him come in," said Lily. "He's nobody to be
afraid of."

Patrick might have been somebody to be afraid

of. Leering and jerking, he came weaving into the storeroom. His smile was brilliant and fiendish, and his eyes saw nothing. He barked and leaped and charged back and forth and back and forth through the floor papers and the soap bars.

"He's tearing everything up!" shouted High Pockets. "Make him stop!"

"He's having a fit!" cried Lily. "It's the disease his father died from."

"A fit," said High Pockets in a frozen tone. He stood rooted.

It was a tense moment. Patrick had seized a strip of the butcher's paper and was rolling on the floor. He was howling, and it appeared that he was trying to eat the paper.

Caught up in this act, Lily ran to Patrick and bent over him. "Son, where are you hurting? Can you tell Mother?"

"You ain't my mother," screamed Patrick. His laugh was horrible, and one of his kicks landed a blow to Lily's stomach.

"He doesn't know you," said High Pockets in a tone of awe. "Do something! Can't you do something?"

Lily discovered that she could still speak. "There's nothing to be done. If this doesn't kill him, I'll get him out of here as soon as it's over. You'd better leave us."

Patrick gave High Pockets such a good send-off

that even Lily was shaken for a moment. When the door had slammed behind High Pockets and she and Patrick had the room to themselves, she punched Patrick in his stomach. "That's for what you did to me."

"I had to scare him so he'd go away," gasped Patrick. "I was out there and I heard what he said. I told you about him, but you didn't listen."

"Get up," ordered Lily. "We've got to get out of here." She could hear High Pockets moving around in an overhead room. He had retreated to his upstairs. "We'll go out the back way," said Lily. "That way we won't run into him again."

"He said we could have the turkey and pie," declared Patrick. He wouldn't leave without them. He had eaten a gouge from one of the pies and selected a whole one still in its baking tin. He thought of how the turkey could be carried back to the camp under the red cedar trees—in a sling made of his undershirt.

Going back across the fields, Lily turned once for a last look at High Pockets' house. The sun was lowering, and in its slanting rays the house looked permanent and decent. Field mice ran chittering through the grasses, and from the camp beneath the trees in the distance there rose a curl of smoke.

At Lily's side, Patrick swung along hugging the pie. He wanted to know why Lily was mad at him.

"I'm not mad at you," said Lily, angry with herself. She was dirty. She was tired and she felt cheapened. At supper, when she joined the others of her family, she ate little and said little. The campfire was cheerful. Patrick and Danny drank canned milk diluted with water.

Still determined to infect his family with the pioneer spirit, Judson said, "You see how it is? You meet all kinds of people when you travel like this, and they're as glad to meet you as you are to meet them. People like that farmer up there in his big house recognize people like us for our worth. We're somebody to envy. That man envies us and wishes he could go with us. That's why he sent us our supper. What was his name, Lily? You didn't tell us his name."

Lily threw the turkey carcass into the fire. It had been picked clean and any other time would have been saved for the next day's soup pot. Feeding on it, the fire sent up fresh sparks.

The wind blew smoke into Lily's face, and it made her eyes water. She could taste her dirt and smell it. She longed for a warm tub bath and a real bed. Anybody who would envy us would either have to be blind or an idiot, she thought. "I think that man said his name was Roy G. Biv," she said.

The dusk was coming. Hurrying to beat it, Lily and her father went to the creek to wash plates and forks. They carried buckets of water back to camp for hands and face scrubbings. Only Danny was brave enough for a full bath in the creek. He came back from it shivering.

The dusk came and then the night, the long night. It was not a glad experience to undress in the darkness of the tent and to sleep on the ground in a bag. The tent was snug and large enough to accommodate five, but the wind blew against its sides, and along toward morning the cold and the dew crept in.

Three

Keeping to their southern and eastern course, the Snows traveled down through Iowa and down and through the hills and hollows and rugged valleys of southern Missouri. They avoided the cities because Judson said anybody could wander around all day gawking at one and wouldn't be any better off when he quit than when he started.

To his scorn of cities Judson added some hearty arguments against campgrounds. "If you need a cabin and electricity and hot and cold running water, you should stay home." Asking for Martha's agreement, he said, "We don't need all those things, do we?"

Martha ducked her head. To the dollar she knew how much money was in the money belt she wore around her waist. "No," she answered. "We don't need all of those things." Riding beside Judson in the car's front seat, she watched the road and looked at the scenes and didn't say very much.

Still soaking in the misery of his private world, Danny kept his corner neat and pretended to read. Lily played the musical comb for Patrick and told him stories. He liked the blood-and-guts kind, so somebody either had to be marched off to the gallows or had to die in the street of gunshot wounds.

In the small towns Martha and Judson went shopping for food. In one town Judson bought some cheap fishing tackle, and every day as soon as camp had been struck jogged off. Usually he came back with a string of perch or sunfish for the supper skillet.

Nights and early mornings on the banks of a little river or a spring were chilly. Noons and afternoons were pleasantly warm. For the birds it was autumn migration time. Early one morning while the Snows were breaking camp the birds came. They came and came and still they came, and Patrick imitated the sound of their passing. "Whew. Whew. Whew."

Lily bent to button his sweater and looked into his happy eyes. She kissed him, and he said, "You smell like fish."

"You don't," said Lily. "You smell like a rose. So today when we stop we're both going to have a bath. A real one. The water won't be too cold. Even if it is, we'll do it real quick and then we'll put our clothes on and run back to the fire. That's how we did it last time. Remember?"

Patrick remembered. "It was cold and you didn't take your clothes off. Only me."

"Because you're not a baby anymore and I'm a lady," explained Lily.

"Arrumph," said Patrick like a little doubting professor. That day he had many complaints. He said he was tired of being Patrick and why couldn't he be somebody else? He said that he had been lied to, that Danny couldn't be his real brother because if he was he wouldn't be so mean to Patrick. He wouldn't pinch Patrick and stick his tongue out at him.

"Danny," said Lily, "don't pinch Patrick anymore and don't stick your tongue out at him again."

Patrick hung on the back of Judson's seat. He said why couldn't Papa make the car go faster so he could get to Florida quicker, that if he was the one doing the driving, it wouldn't take him so long.

"This gasoline nag will go as fast as I want it to go and no faster," said Judson. "Sit down, Patrick."

Patrick returned to his seat. He said that he had heard the story about Painless Potter who was a dentist when he wasn't busy being a train robber a hundred times and didn't want to hear it again. "Why was he a dentist? He didn't have to be one. He had lots of money."

"He liked to pull people's teeth and hear them scream," said Lily.

"Did he have any children?"

"I don't know. I didn't ask him."

"What did he do with all that money he stole?"

"He bought himself some new clothes and went to town and had a good time."

"He bought some clothes before he went to town? How could he do that? Where was the store?"

"At Rhubarb Gulch."

"I don't know where that is."

"Neither do I."

With his tongue, Patrick counted his teeth. "When Painless went to town and had a good time, did he go by himself?"

"No," said Lily. "He had a girl friend."

"What was her name?"

"Nell."

"Nell what?"

"Nell Plenty Quick."

"That was her name? Nell Plenty Quick?"

"I think so."

"Why?"

"Because she got all of the money away from Painless plenty quick and ran away with it plenty quick."

Patrick said he didn't care where Nell Plenty Quick went with the money, and he didn't want to hear any more stories about Painless Potter either. "If you tell me any more stories about him, I'm going to throw up," he said. "All over Danny."

"Gag him," said Danny.

"Gag yourself," said Lily.

The car hit a rut in the road, coughed, and gave a little lurch. Judson righted it. "Shut up back there!" he roared. "If you don't shut up, you'll all get out and walk. Do you think it's any fun for me, driving a bunch of lunatics to Florida and having to listen to all that wrangling at the same time?"

"Jud," soothed Martha, "you're tired. We're all a little tired. Let's find a nice place and stop early today. I need to do a little washing, and if we stop early, the clothes will dry before dark."

"I am not tired," said Judson, but when he got out of the car forty-five minutes later, he leaned against one of its fenders and took in a long breath. As he unpacked the trailer, he stopped several times and stood in the cautious attitude of one waiting for some inner disturbance to pass.

He will never let himself be tired, thought Lily. She put Patrick in Danny's care and went with Martha to do the washing in a shallow campsite stream. The slow-moving water was clear and cool, not cold.

Kneeling on rough, bankside stones, Martha and Lily bent to their task. There were stains in the clothes that would not come out even with repeated soapings, and Martha said, "I should have remembered we'd have to do this. We need a washboard."

"Yes," said Lily, angry with one of Judson's shirts,

angrier with its owner, angry with everything. What was needed was not anything so down-and-out as a washboard but a machine. And back there in the trees there shouldn't be a tent but a house with a polished door and white ruffles showing at its windows. All over the world there were men who provided homes like that for their wives and children. How was it her father never had? He was a man. He knew how to do things. He wasn't lazy. But the things he did never came to anything. He ran after his ideas the way a child runs after a balloon. If there was a river to be crossed and there wasn't a boat—well, don't worry, folks. I'll nail these two logs together, and that will be our boat.

The boat always sank. The balloon was never caught. The house with the polished door and the white ruffles showing at its windows always belonged to somebody else.

Lily gave her father's shirt a final, hard twist and slung it into the waiting basket. She and her mother hung the clothes on bushes and spread them out on the grass to dry. There was sun.

On the way back to the tent, Martha stooped to pick a flower. She said she thought she would fry some apples for supper.

Patrick and Danny had eaten two of Martha's apple hoard. Each blamed this crime on the other.

Martha looked at both of them, made her lips thin, and looked away. Her dress and Lily's were damp in front from waist to hemline, and Patrick, seeing this, clapped his hands to his cheeks. "Oh, you had a bath and you're all wet. Was the water cold? I wasn't there, so why didn't you take your clothes off? Mama, you're both ladies, so why didn't you take your clothes off?"

Martha set one of the camp stools up close to the door of the tent and sat on it. She drew her skirt around her knees and regarded her water-puckered hands. "I used to be a lady. I remember when I was. Did I ever tell you children that at the time I met your father I was engaged to marry a cattle king?"

"Papa said that man you were engaged to worked in a hardware store," said Danny.

"He owned it," said Martha. "It was one of his hobbies. He had a new car, and we went riding every Sunday afternoon. When he took me out to dine, we always ate at the finest restaurants. My aunt went along to chaperone. She was a lovely lady herself. She adored me. I know I broke her heart when I broke off my engagement to the cattle king."

"You said she was hag number one and didn't care who you married as long as you did it to somebody so she wouldn't have to take care of you anymore," said Danny.

"I had beautiful clothes then," said Martha. "My aunt bought them for me. And she made me take care of my complexion and my hands."

"I had to eat that apple to show Patrick it wasn't poisoned," said Danny. "He thought they were all poisoned, so I ate mine first to show him they weren't."

Papa is right, thought Lily, sorting through a duffel bag. We are lunatics. She handed Patrick his towel but knew better than to trust him with the bar of soap. On the way to the creek he shuddered and shook and said cold bath water always gave him cold dots.

"What's this about cold dots?" said Lily. "Something new? What are cold dots?"

"Those goose things you get when you're cold," moaned Patrick.

"The water's not cold enough to give you goose pimples," said Lily. "If it does, the sun will warm you up."

Patrick had his bath and, wrapped in his towel, streaked away to the warmth of sun and the safety of camp.

Clothed except for her shoes, standing in the creek water, Lily considered her wilderness bathhouse. At the turn in the creek there was dark, overhanging tree growth, and, keeping to the center of the stream, Lily started toward it. There were small stones on the creek bottom, and these were a nuisance. The water slid along at a fair rate.

At the curve in the creek, Lily waded to shore and bent to set her shoes down. Wind stirred the tops of the shore trees and fluttered their branches. Lily straightened and looked up and saw her father. He was sitting well back from the creek bank in a patch of shade. He had his back against a tree trunk and his head was on his knees. Lily thought that he might be napping and carelessly called out to him. "Papa?"

Her father did not stir. Lily left the creek and walked toward him. When she reached him, she knelt beside him. "Papa, are you asleep?"

Her father raised his head. His eyes searched her face.

"Papa," said Lily, "you were asleep."

"Oh, Lily, it's you," said her father. From the woods on the opposite side of the creek there came a wild, soaring cackle, and from Judson's mouth there came a question, "What was that?"

"Nothing," answered Lily, surprised. "A bird." Her father knew birds. He could imitate them. "Papa, you're still asleep," said Lily.

"I was a little short on breath and had to rest for a few minutes," responded Judson. He passed a hand over his face. "Don't tell your mother."

In the silence there came again the cackling of the unseen bird. "I won't tell her," said Lily. Holding her towel and the bar of soap, she stood and looked at the creek. "I was going to take a bath, but with you here I can't."

Her father's smile was faint. Carrying his fishing

rod, he walked away from the creek, leaving Lily to her bath. He left his favorite hat, the one with the green feather in its band, on the creek bank and didn't miss it until the next morning. Lily went after it, and when she handed it to him he stuck it on his head and gave its brim a tweak. Grinning, he said, "You know how to read a road map?"

"No," said Lily.

Her father handed her a map. "Just follow the green line, the one I made with my crayon." He had trouble with the loading of the trailer. Twice he stopped to rest. When it was time to start out, he climbed into the passenger side of the car's front seat. "You drive," he said to Martha.

"Oh no," said Martha. "That's your responsibility. Come on, Jud. Move over. I don't feel like jokes this morning." She wore a blue jacket and had tied a blue scarf around her head. Standing in the chilly sunlight, she looked like a schoolgirl. With the help of a South Dakota cowboy, a young swaggart who smoldered for automobiles and who respected married ladies, she had learned how to drive. At the time it had been something to gloat over. It had been proof to Judson that there was more to her than just being his little-woman pet. But flat prairie was one thing. That road out there with the swells in it was quite another. "I don't feel like driving," said Martha. "Come on now, Jud. Let's get started."

Judson was playing at being Husband on His Day Off. Lazily he scratched himself. He yawned. "I didn't sleep much last night, and this morning I'm tired, so if we're going to go anywhere today you'll have to get us there. You drive."

"Driving makes me nervous," objected Martha.

"Drive," said Judson. He pulled his hat down over his eyes and pretended to snore.

Glaring her displeasure and defeat, Martha stalked around to the driver's side of the car and stood there yanking at her head scarf. There was angry color in her face. She kicked at the dirt and blew her breath.

Preparing for the day's long drive, Lily, Danny, and Patrick had climbed into the car's back seat. Danny and Patrick began to arrange their personal plunder around them. Danny couldn't find his nail file and accused Patrick of swiping it. It was too early for a fight. They bickered as if the outcome didn't matter.

"What'd you do with my nail file?"

"I haven't got it."

"You've got it. Give it back."

"I told you I haven't got it."

"You have too."

"I have not."

Lily closed her ears to this wrangling. Like the evicted tenant on moving day, the one who doesn't want to go and knows he cannot stay, she looked out at the deserted camp. It was as she and her family had found it: neat, impersonal, no trace of anything human anywhere, soundless except for the singsonging of autumn insects.

Four

The Snows' travel that day took them out of Missouri
and into Tennessee. Within sight of the Mississippi
River, Judson had Martha stop the car long enough
to rearrange the seating so that Lily would ride in
the front seat beside Martha and he would share the
back one with Patrick and Danny.

It was Indian summer, that serene and secretive
time of year that drifts between the yellow days of
the real summer and the red ones of fall. The air
was alive with warmth and a tingle in it, but only
Judson spoke of it, and only he looked at the Mississippi, that old twisted river, more than once.

Patrick whined to be taken into the front seat with
Lily, and hid his white face in his sweater when
Martha slapped him across his mouth and said, "No!"
Forlornly he wept, and after a minute Lily said, "He
didn't deserve that, Mama."

"He's rotten spoiled and it's your fault," flamed

59

Martha. "You give him everything he wants."

"He don't know what he wants," said Danny. "But he comes by that honest. It runs in the family. Let's go, or are we going to sit here all day?"

"I ought to let you sit here all day," said Martha, all puffed up. To start the drive across Tennessee took all of her attention and most of Lily's. Martha made mistakes, which she blamed on the state of Tennessee. She said that she was going to write to its governor about its roads, that there were too many curves in them, which might be all right for a two-hundred-pound truck driver but was hard for a person like herself who had never weighed over a hundred and five pounds in her life. She said, "How big is this state anyway?"

Lily consulted the road map but couldn't find where it said how big Tennessee was. She couldn't consult her father. He was asleep, and she said, "It's big."

"Well, I don't know why anybody would want to live here," said Martha. Her head scarf now hung in a string around her neck, her hair was wilted, and her lipstick was smudged. In harsh tones she began to tell Lily of her first married years. "We lived up over a pool hall. We had two rooms and had to climb two flights of stairs to get to them. I can still remember how dark they were and how they smelled. Smelly. I don't think I ever told you that you were born in a room over a pool hall, have I?"

"No," answered Lily. And said, "Papa's asleep. He said he didn't get much rest last night."

"Neither did I," said Martha. "And now here he hands me the whole family to take care of. I'll tell you something, Lily. Your father has pulled some idiotic stunts on me, but this one is the craziest yet. Trekking across half of the United States like a bunch of hoboes. I'll tell you something, Lily. If it weren't for you children I wouldn't be sitting here behind this wheel. But that's the way it's always been. It's always been I've had to do things I didn't want to do because of you children. Because of you I've never thought for more than five minutes about quitting. That's what my parents did to me when I was eight. They quit, and one went one way and the other went the other. They forgot about me. That's what I haven't wanted to happen to you."

Lily wished to be suddenly, temporarily deaf. She thought about that old Breathless Boy, the one who had given her his elk's tooth. He would never stash her in two rooms up over a pool hall. He had a long curved nose with a bulb on its end and talked as if somebody had wound him up with a key. Lily shuddered.

The Snows were then in what Lily thought must be cotton country, flat and black. They stopped for gas and oil, and Martha went into the station's rest room to get money from the money belt.

Thirty minutes later the sun disappeared and the air turned gray. Judson roused to look out. There were dry leaves in the ditches.

It began to rain, big silvery drops splashing against the car windows and hood at first but then turning into a real trash mover. As if a hole had been punched in it, the sky opened and the water came down in sheets, filling the hollows in the road and beating against the sides of the car.

There was trouble. There were loops in the road, and after taking several of these the trailer began to fishtail, to weave back and forth. Each time it did this, it took a longer time to straighten out. Judson was awake and said its trouble was either a loose bolt or shifted weight. He said, "Speed up and it'll straighten out."

Instead Martha pulled the car over to a stop. "Get out and fix it, Jud. You'll have to get out and fix whatever it is that's wrong."

Judson got out of the car and ran back to the trailer.

"He might need some help," said Lily.

"Out in the middle of nowhere," said Martha. "We're always out in the middle of nowhere."

Lily got out of the car and slammed its door behind her. The rain was cold. There was half a gale behind it.

Judson had climbed up onto the trailer's hitch. He had pushed the tarpaulin to one side and was tugging at the tent. He had to shout to make himself heard. "Get back in the car! There's no sense in both of us drowning!"

"It isn't just us that'll drown!" cried Lily. "It's everything!" She had had almost no Bible training but had heard about Judgment Day, and from time to time during her younger life had vaguely wondered what would happen to her when it came. Once as a small child in a Wyoming town she had proudly delivered a May basket to an old, red-eyed woman and had been told that the Day was just around the corner. As a child she had seen the basket as a work of art, a violent-pink, homemade crepe paper affair filled with secondhand jelly beans and sprigs of dusty field flowers. As one grown older she remembered the basket for the hideous affair that it had been. The woman had shrieked her hatred of it, and Lily had been obliged to sit and listen to what happens to snippy children on Judgment Day. It hadn't been made clear to her how she was snippy and whether she would drown or burn for her sin when the day of reckoning came. Now the thought flashed through her mind that maybe it had come, that maybe God intended to drown both her and the state of Tennessee.

Tugging and pulling at the trailer's freight, her father was half in and half out of the trailer. The wind stole his hat and sailed it away. The wind whipped a no-nonsense order from his mouth. "Get back in the car, Lily! Go on!"

She was soaked, and Martha said she hoped the car's upholstery wouldn't be ruined. Lily took her shoes off, rolled her window down, and dumped water from them. Except for his lost hat and his wetness she didn't, at first, notice anything in particular about her father when he returned to the car.

"I suppose everything is ruined," said Martha. As a towel, she offered her scarf.

"It wasn't a loose bolt," said Judson, mopping his face. "It was the tent. It had shifted around some. I fixed it. Let's go." He shook water from his hair. His voice was thin. It sounded squeezed, as though it came from a tube.

Martha started the car. "I'm glad I thought to put the flour and sugar in jars."

"Nothing is ruined," said Judson, and Lily turned and looked at him. His lips were tinged blue, and there was pallor in his face. It looked drained, and he was pulling his breath in and letting it out as if he and it were in a struggle to see which would get the next one. He had drawn into his corner and his head was back.

A little shocked and a little frightened, Lily said, "Patrick, give Papa your sweater."

"It won't fit him," said Patrick.

Lily reached back and in two yanks had the sweater. To drape it over her father's chest was a long reach; she had to stand on her knees. His half smile thanked her. He didn't open his eyes.

The wind had blown itself out. The rain was slackening. Presently it stopped, and now, from both sides of the highway, from the sodden land there rose a mist.

Facing the road, staring through the windshield at the road, Lily faced uncertainty and risk. She wanted to grab her mother's arm and in a whisper say, "Stop. There is something scary going on with Papa, and before it gets any bigger you had better have a look at it."

Her mother was the risk. She might look at the scary calmly and decide whether it was something or nothing or she might jump from the car and, with smoke pouring from her ears, tear off looking for anything to dive into or hide behind. She could live in two rooms up over a pool hall. She could live in a house so close to the railroad tracks that it shook when the trains rumbled past. She could stand behind Papa's grocery counter and hold a queenly conversation with the worst bleary-eyed bowlegs ever to stagger down Main Street, but she did these things only because somebody told her to do them. About the only important thing she had ever done on her own was learning how to drive. Mama's somebody was Papa. Mama had never faced the dangers of growing up.

Tasting her uncertainty, chewing on it, Lily watched the road and every so often stole a look at her father. He slept. The color in his face and lips returned. He woke and said, "Where are we?" And it wasn't the question of a sick man. It was the question of an interested one.

Lily rattled the road map and, showing her father, jabbed at a spot on it with her finger. She had spent the better part of the day worrying and there was nothing to worry about. Was there?

Her father's behavior said no. He pointed out the surrounding hills and an abandoned tannery standing on the bank of a stream. He wanted to stop and look at it, but Martha said she didn't like old buildings, that spiders and snakes lived in them.

The Snows found their night's campsite just beyond the tannery, and after the tent had been raised, Judson took Danny and Patrick on a scouting trip. They came back with armloads of firewood.

"I saw some fairy lamps," said Patrick.

"They were toadstools," said Danny.

"Papa said they were fairy lamps," said Patrick.

Judson had a handful of dirt and showed it to Martha and Lily. "This is the kind of soil I hope to find on our land in Florida."

"We're going to have us a farm," said Patrick, loving this delicious news. He snatched a potato peeling from the pan in Lily's lap and ate it.

"A farm," said Martha, and dropped her paring knife into her pan of sliced onions. Her eyes glittered. "A farm," she said. "So we can all work together. What will we grow on it, Judson?"

"Anything that will bring us a living," answered Judson. He had given up playing Husband on His Day Off. There was the supper fire to kindle and feed, more wood to gather, and water buckets to be filled.

In a skillet, Lily mixed the onions and potatoes and set them to frying. I will not, she thought, live on a farm. I will not, she thought, be a farmer's daughter and hang on that old red gate waiting for the cows to come home. Or stand there waiting for Mr. Future Farmer to come flapping up in his rusty Ford so I can hear all about how he's going to buy a swell new truck as soon as the crops come in. And hear all about how many acres he and Uncle Horace planted that day. How, before long, he will have a place of his own. How, come Saturday night, he would like to take me to town to see *The Clutching Hand*, a swell movie about a magician.

Lily had seen *The Clutching Hand* three times. She stirred the potato and onion mixture. She allowed it to become too crisp, and at supper Danny said, "When you get married, it had better be to somebody who can cook or somebody with enough money so he can hire his cooking done. You sure can't do it."

"The man lucky enough to get me for his wife will thank his angels," said Lily. "He'll bring a cook with him when he comes to get me." She was barefooted because her everyday shoes were still wet from their afternoon soaking. She owned two pairs and was saving her better ones. When she went with Patrick to see the fairy lamps, the cold of the forest floor nipped at her feet. On the way back to camp she told Patrick that there would come a day when she would own fifty pairs of shoes.

The Snows had visitors that evening, a man and his wife who made their camp downstream. The man said they were from Georgia and were on their way to Memphis to see a new grandson. He said he was a doctor but for the Snows to keep that quiet because he never mixed business with pleasure. His hair was an orange hood except around his ears, where it curled white. When he gave his name and that of his wife's, it sounded to Lily as if he wasn't sure what they were. "I'm Doctuh Colvin, and this is my better half? Her name is Geddie?"

"You talk funny," said Patrick.

"That's my Georgia accent," twinkled the doctor. He looked like a recent graduate from a health club.

Geddie smelled of garlic and had a jolly laugh. "Don't let the doctuh fool you about that mixing up his business with his pleasure. His business is his pleasure and his pleasure is his business."

Judson shook hands with the doctor and freshened the fire. He offered coffee to the Colvins. They said they did not drink coffee, that they drank only herb teas and vegetable or fruit juices.

"My husband is a naturopathic physician," said Geddie.

"How nice," said Martha.

"So we live by the laws of nature," said Geddie. "We couldn't live any other way. We don't drink coffee, and we pay strict attention to what we eat. We are never sick. To nourish and keep our organs, tissues, and cells clean we eat cottage cheese and fresh, raw fruits and vegetables."

"We eat lots of apples," said Martha. "And Judson believes in barley soup when one of the children gets sick." She did not say that when Judson rushed home to put the soup pot on, she immediately found an excuse that took her out of the sick room, out of the house, out of the sight and smell of ailment.

The doctor said he approved of apples and home-made soups. Twice he and Geddie rose to go, and twice they were urged to stay a while longer. Judson wanted to hear more about the doctor's healing-by-nature methods.

So the flattered doctor hooked his thumbs in his

belt and talked. The fire burned low, and Judson replenished it. The doctor had the gift of gab and didn't tire easily, but one by one the tired Snows, all but Judson, went off to their beds. Martha left the door flap to the tent open.

Lily's feet were dirty, and she didn't care. She slept. And woke to raise up and look out. The Colvins had gone. The camp was hushed, but still its fire burned. Judson sat beside it gazing at a sprinkling of stars hanging in the east.

Lily left the tent and went outside, shivering a little because her nightgown wasn't enough protection against the coolness. Her father invited her to share the warmth of his fire. Beyond its circle of light there were trees standing tall in the darkness.

Judson said everything should be as simple as a tree.

"Is there any coffee left?" asked Lily.

"There was," answered her father. "I threw it out. We shouldn't drink coffee. I'm not going to buy any more. We'll drink herb and cereal drinks."

"Mama likes coffee," said Lily.

"Your mother likes candy," observed Judson. "But she shouldn't eat it. If I wasn't around to tell her when to stop eating it, she'd stuff herself with it every day. I have to watch her. Since the day I married her I've had to do that. She doesn't know how to take care of herself." His next comment was light. It wandered. "I keep thinking, suppose some noon I decide to go to the zoo instead of eating my lunch, and a lion decides I'm his lunch?"

"I don't think there will be any zoos where we're going," said Lily.

"I'm supposing," mused her father. "Suppose there is a zoo where we're going. Or suppose some night when I'm on my way home I fall down a manhole or a horse bites me and I get laid up for a while. Then what? Then who would take charge, do you suppose?"

"Oh, suppose, suppose," said Lily, and went back to the tent and her sleeping bag. She lay with a hand tucked under a cheek and after a while remembered a childhood trick that had usually helped when she was faced with an unpleasant or bad truth. She used it now. It didn't happen, she told herself. I didn't see what I saw today. It was just the cold and the rain that made Papa look sick. He's not sick.

She hadn't worn the trick out. It still worked.

Five

There was a day in Tennessee when the Snows stood on a mountain, but since he was down to one, Judson had changed his mind about throwing his hat into the wind. The wind and leaf color said that the southern fall was seriously under way, and Judson was excited. He had taken over the driving of the car and said that he didn't have time to chase after his hat and couldn't afford to lose it either. So it was "All aboard, folks! Step lively there! Georgia is next, and then we'll be home."

In Georgia there were red clay hills and side roads of red clay. Tin signs nailed to roadside trees advertised patent medicines, Orange Crush, and Coca-Cola.

The Snows' canned milk supply was finished, so in a crossroads village they ate a café breakfast. The waitress, whose curled lip said she just knew that she needn't expect a tip for her services, slung the food onto the table. She had a deep-South accent. "No, honey, that's not cereal. It's grits. Well, sugar, grits aren't a thing but ground-up corn. They're painless. Some people even like them. I got a name for them—Georgia ice cream."

"You say your words different," said Patrick.

"Lambie," said the waitress, "you got your English and I got mine."

Judson ordered everybody to eat the grits. Lily said hers were interesting. To her they were about as interesting as a doorknob, but she thought she should say that because the waitress had lumpy legs shaped like those of a piano stool.

The waitress said the trees out there were pecan, and that she had a Florida uncle who made a good living at raising peanuts. "I went to see him once but didn't get to see much of anything except peanuts, and if I'd have wanted to see what they looked like I could have stayed right here. So I can't tell you what Florida's like. Uncle tried to put me to driving his mules, so I came on back here."

Judson grew thoughtful. On the way to Florida he talked about peanuts, saying how good hot roasted ones tasted on a cold night. He didn't have a gold nugget but said he would just bet his last one that there wasn't much to making peanut butter.

Listening to her father ramble, Lily sat beside him holding a road map of Florida. She kept her eyes on the passing scenery and wondered what Florida's marrying age was. She drew a mental picture of Florida men. Some looked like Indians and some like farmers. The farmers had heads shaped like bullets and couldn't find anything to talk about except to repeat what the man on the radio had said last Sunday night.

The map in Lily's hand told her that she might as well give up any hope of seeing the Atlantic Ocean, at least for the time being. After more red clay hills such as those in Georgia the road settled down to running through flatwoods. There were stands of pines, palmetto thickets, and oaks draped in Spanish moss. There were roadside patches of yellow partridge peas and scarlet wallflowers. There were towns. Signs announced such attractions as Herbie's Pit Barbecue and Viola's Dine and Dance.

In the car's back seat, Martha ate stale licorice and tried to keep peace between Danny and Patrick. She pointed out things of interest. "Oh, look at that quaint house. Isn't it quaint?"

"We've lived in lots quainter," said Danny, "but when we did, that's not what you called them."

"And look at those yellow and red flowers," said Martha. "I wonder what they are."

"Where are the oranges?" cried Patrick. "I want to see the oranges. Papa, stop! I want to get out and see the oranges. I want to pick one."

"If and when somebody sees a tree with oranges on it, I'll stop," said Judson, and drove on. His one experience with farming had been a boy's backyard patch that had produced only a handful of skinny carrots and a bitter cabbage the size of a man's bowling ball. Never in the whole of his life had he given two thoughts to where peanuts grew or how, yet now he began to talk about the merits of peanut farming as if they might be aroused memories, something he had forgotten and come back to. "We're going to work mules on our farm. As soon as I get the house built I'm going to see somebody in town about pairing a pair."

The town of Sweet Root was certainly not something somebody had just thought of yesterday. It sprawled in all directions. Its center street was dotted with immense live oaks, and its hotel was the kind that went out of style in the nineteen twenties. Bragg's One Stop Service Station was across the street from the hotel.

The Snows pulled into the station, and an attendant strolled out. He said he was Billy Bragg, and riveted his first attention on Lily. "How are you?"

"Oh," said Lily, "I'm just hotsy-totsy."

Billy shifted his gaze to take in the car's rear-seat passengers and its contents. "Looks like you've been traveling."

"We have, but we're finished with it now," said Judson. "We own some land around here somewhere."

"Is it in Sweet Root?" asked Billy.

"It's about five miles west of here," said Judson.

"Five miles west of here is nothing but wild," informed Billy. "Nobody lives out there but Waite Cody and his old buddy. They're free spirits, that's what they'll tell you if you ask them why. Waite owns about half of Sweet Root, but he don't spend much time in it. He likes it out where the turtles and the quail live."

"Our property is bounded on the west by Sweet Root Falls," said Judson.

"I know the Falls," said Billy. "But if you want to know where your property is exactly, you'd better get ahold of Waite. He's got him a place upriver at the Falls, and he'll see you when you go in. You mightn't see him, but he'll see you."

Another attendant, a woman, came from the station and asked Billy if he had given the Snows a Sweet Root visitor sticker. She addressed Billy as Private. "Private, have you given these folks one of our visitor stickers?"

"No'm," said Billy, mopping bugs and dirt from the car's windshield. "I haven't had time yet. Anyway, they're not visitors. They've come to stay. They're going to live at the Falls."

"Is that right," exclaimed the woman, and shoved her hand in to Judson so he could shake it. "Welcome to Sweet Root. I'm Pauline Bragg and Billy here is my son. Well now, we're happy to add you people to our population. So you're from South Dakota. What's there?"

"Some hills," said Judson. "Some prairie. Some Indians."

Pauline stuck her head in past Judson's shoulder to smile at Martha. "My, you're pretty. Are these three young ones here yours?"

"Yes," answered Martha. She loved a compliment.

"We got good kids here," said Pauline. "They behave, but when one of them gets out of line, whichever one of us catches him shows him the mistakes of his ways, and then we go tell his mama or his daddy and he gets showed again. Mrs. Reed is our school principal. She's strict."

Billy had finished with the windshield and went around to stand beside his mother. He was eager to get some of his statistics out of the way. "Ma got me this place after I came back from the Army. It about ruint me to do anything but pump gas. I hurt my back when the Army had me. I kept telling the sergeant how it pained me to pick up cigarette butts, and he kept telling me if I'd exercise my back more it wouldn't hurt. So every Saturday morning he'd put me to picking up cigarette butts. I am here to tell you I mortally despise cigarette butts. If a general or anybody like that was coming, the sergeant would make me go over the grounds twice to make sure I hadn't missed any. No general ever came except one. His red eyes looked into my red eyes and he said, 'Soldier, you're a soldier, so stand like one.' Nobody believes a bad back."

Pauline started to describe Sweet Root Falls but cut it short, and instead gave instructions on how to get there. "You'll see how it is when you get there. To get there you go on down this street till you see a house that's got green bottles around its flower beds. That's the schoolhouse. Your kids go to school, don't they?"

"When they run out of excuses they do," said Martha. "All except the smallest one here."

"Well, anyway," said Pauline, "that house where you'll see the green bottles is the schoolhouse. Turn right there and follow the road on out until you see the Falls. You'll think you've missed them, but keep going and you'll see them. Waite Cody will be out there to show you where your land is. He knows it all, backwards and forwards."

Martha said she was sure Mr. Cody would be helpful, and went to the station's rest room. She came back and invited the rest of the Snows to go with her to a store to shop for food.

"You can leave the car here," said Billy. "I'll watch it." He did more than watch it. When the Snows returned to it, they saw that it had been shampooed and that a Welcome to Sweet Root sticker had been attached to its windshield. Billy said the wash job was a present, and grandly opened the car door for Lily. "I'll be seeing you," he said.

"Sure," said Lily.

Billy wasn't ready to let it go at that. He leaned toward her. The whites of his eyes were startlingly white. "I used to be a terrible liar."

"I forgive you," said Lily.

"There isn't a thing wrong with my back," said Billy. "I could pick this car up and run it around the block and not even breathe hard."

Judson had started the car, and Lily said, "We've got to go. Good-bye."

"Oh no," said Billy. "Not good-bye." But he closed the car door and stood back. A duck had come out from behind the filling station, and he took something from his pocket and fed it.

Before noon that day the Snows found what Judson said was their land. This hollow in the woodland had to be it, he said. His documents told him so, he said. He scooped up a handful of dirt and rubbed his face in it. He tasted it, and even Danny laughed to see his blackened lips.

Patrick was beside himself. He squealed his excitement. "Is this going to be our place? Are we going to live here? Lily, are we going to live here? Lily, talk to me!"

"Yes, this is our place and we're going to live here," said Lily. Listening to the silence, she felt that she was standing on the rim of the world and that if she took a wrong step she might fall off.

Under a wide sky this wide glade, all shades of green, lay strange and aloof. There was nothing intimate about it, nothing that said, "Welcome." The Falls didn't look real. Its water frothed white where it spilled over flat rock plateaus with a drop of a foot or so between them. It was the color of light syrup where it left the rocks to become a part of a narrow river and a series of bankside pools.

Some of the land had been cleared and stood in sun. In shade, resting on flat ground, was a concrete house foundation. Running up to it was a dirt road.

The foundation looked fairly new, and Judson was certain that his half brother had built it or had had it built. "Scott was going to live here," he said.

Judson had come home. He was wild for the land, his land, and couldn't get to his plans for it fast enough. "We'll take up where Scott left off. We'll use the foundation to set our house on, and back here I'll make a pen for the mules. Out here is where we'll grow our peanuts. I wonder if the power company in Sweet Root will run some lines for electricity out here. I'll go in and see about that first thing Monday morning. But until we can get some power we can use the river for our springhouse. The water is cold enough to keep food from spoiling. Do you remember our springhouse in Wyoming, Martha? How we put our meat and milk in jars and lowered them into the water?"

Martha pressed fingers to her temples. "Jud, don't you think we'd better wait for that Cody person to come and tell us we're in the right spot before we start digging in here and making plans? The letter from the attorney didn't say a word about Scott ever having been here. We might be in the wrong place."

Judson shook his land documents. "We're in the right spot. I don't need a prophet to tell me that. All I need is these. Now let's see. It takes lumber to build a house, and I can handle that all right. I can fell trees. I know how to swing an ax. Let me think, let me think. We'll have a log house. I can raise one, I know I can. Where's some paper? Danny, get Papa some paper and a pencil from the trailer. I'm going to draw a house plan. Martha, how many rooms do you think you'll want?"

"Five," said Martha, small and helpless and re-signed.

Tired of chasing a quail, Patrick came back panting to the cold lunch spread out on a picnic cloth. He said, "That fat bird runs too quick."

Lily left him with Judson and Martha and walked away from the Falls and the camp. A log house, she thought. A peanut farm. Mules. Did I ever say to myself that here even the donkey might sing sweetly? Well, he won't. I'm the donkey, and you don't hear me singing, do you? Who could in a place like this? Why did I promise Mama that I wouldn't leave, that I would stay? Because I'm a donkey.

The forest had animal eyes and animal ears, and from their hiding places the eyes looked out at Lily. They saw the scornful twist of her mouth. They watched her run and stop, and saw her raise her clenched hands and shake her angry fists at the sky.

Where there was no sun, the forest dripped with moisture. On their thorny bushes the haws were red. There was a day mist, and out of it stepped a giant of a man followed by a short one. The giant wore a bush hat, khaki shirt and trousers, and swash-buckler boots. He looked as if he had been born in the woods. The short one watched everything the giant did.

The giant stood in Lily's path. He almost bowed to her as he swept his hat off and told her that he was Waite Cody and that his companion went by the name of Doe.

"La," said Lily. Because there was something dis-turbing in Waite's direct gaze it took her a second to remember that she was Lily Snow and to say so.

Doe stood off to one side and didn't try very hard to hide what was at once clear to Lily: that he looked upon her as an intruder. "Waite and me never thought to see any of Scott's folks come here," he said. "But then he never gave us a chance to talk to him much. He'd come and work and then he'd go away again. He was many weeks and dollars getting that foundation built. You say you've got little brothers? I hope they won't throw rocks at the turtles."

Lily said she didn't think Danny and Patrick would throw rocks at the turtles.

On the way to the Falls and the Snows' camp, Doe darted back and forth and around Waite, parting the pathway underbrush to make the going easier.

The tent was up, but except for Judson the camp was deserted. Martha had gone exploring with Danny and Patrick.

Judson showed Waite the land documents. He said he was wondering about the quality of the Falls' water. Waite said it had been checked by the county health department and found to be of good quality. He suggested a walk out to locate the Snows' land boundary lines, and he and Judson and Doe set out. They were gone the better part of an hour. When they came back, Judson excused himself and went to the tent and stayed.

"I don't think your daddy is feeling any too good,"

said Waite. "So Doe and I will be on our way."

"Are we in the right place?" asked Lily.

"It couldn't be righter," said Waite, and this time when he took his hat off to her he actually bowed. His head wasn't shaped like a bullet, and he didn't look like any Indian Lily had known. Watching him swing away, she wondered about his age.

She did not wonder if her father was sick. She saw that he was. She found him lying sprawled on top of his sleeping bag. On her knees beside him, she said, "Papa."

Her father's face was pale, glistening pale. He turned his head and his eyes met hers. "It's nothing to get excited about, Lily. I've been living with it for a long time."

Afraid, Lily said, "What is it?"

Her father sat up and with his sleeve wiped his face. "It's something left over from when I was a kid."

The tent was green, and the light seeping through its ceiling and walls tinged everything an eerie green.

"It's just another nuisance," said Judson. "It takes my breath sometimes, and then I have to sit down or lay down, but I get over it. You see? I'm over it now. Have Cody and his man gone?"

"Yes," answered Lily.

Her father stood and straightened his clothing. "We're in the right place. Did Cody tell you?"

"Yes," said Lily. She looked at her green hands and said, "You should see a doctor."

"So I could turn into an invalid," said Judson. "No thanks. That's what happened to my mother."

Lily sat back and regarded her green legs without seeing them. "What about Mama?"

"What about her," said Judson.

"I don't know," said Lily, groping. "I don't know what about her. I just said what about her."

Her father had gone to the doorway of the tent and was peering out. With his back to Lily he said, "Your mother runs from anybody who is sick. Not that I am, but she'd think I was if I told her I don't feel good at times, so I don't tell her. This comes and goes." There was a plea in Judson's easy tone, but he didn't speak it. He left the tent, and presently Lily heard him calling to Martha and the boys as they trudged back into camp. "What did you see? A turkey? A wild one? Are you sure?"

"And a whale," screamed Patrick.

"It was not a whale, it was a turtle," shouted Danny.

Lily rose and went outside. The colors of the afternoon were brilliant and peaceful, but Danny and Patrick weren't having any part of peace. They were squaring off, preparing to fight, and Judson was between them trying to stave off the hostilities. "Boys, don't fight. What difference does it make whether it was a turtle or a whale? Maybe it was both."

"He threw mud on me," cried Danny.

"Because he made me fall down," shrieked Patrick.

Bewildered, Judson said, "Boys, boys."

And bitterly Martha said, "Talk, talk. That's all you know, and it doesn't do any good. They act like a pair of savages, and there's no sense in it. Can't you do something about it, Jud?"

Judson made an appeal. "Boys, I want you to stop fighting. You're brothers."

Contemptuously Martha said, "Oh," and with a toss of her head lit out for the woods.

Judson looked at Lily, and she looked straight back. She rose from her stool. "Go with Mama and let me take care of this."

"You can't," said her father.

"I can," said Lily, and, when Judson had gone, marched out and seized Danny by his shirt and Patrick by an ear. "I want you to fight. Go on. Ball up your fists. Hit each other. Gouge each other's eyes out. Kill each other. Fight!"

Danny said, "Aw," and backed off. Lily hauled him back. "No, you're going to fight. Go on. Hit Patrick. I want you to hit him. Break his leg. Sock him in the jaw. You hate him, so kill him."

"He steals my stuff and hides it, and he's so dirty!" screamed Danny.

"Because she's a girl," answered Judson, and handed Danny the lunch sack and the thermos jug.

Patrick put up a howl when he was told he would have to stay at home. He said that his organs and tissues were already clean and strong, but ate a few peaches. He said he wasn't a washerwoman and if Lily wanted his socks to be clean she could wash them. He sat on the bank of the river and watched Lily and Martha do the washing.

Lily cleaned the tent and watched the woods. She told herself that she wasn't watching for anything in particular, yet she got out the family hairbrush and put her hair up.

Waite Cody and Doe came, and Patrick danced out to meet them. "Papa and Danny went to chop logs for our new house, and Papa wouldn't let me go because I'm too little," he said. He displayed the bruises on his arms and the ones on his cheeks. "Lily made Danny and me fight and this is what he did to me but I won," he bragged.

Doe said the important thing in a fight was to remember to keep the dukes up, and gave Patrick a brief boxing lesson, showing him how to fend off an opponent's slugs with knotted fists. He held the tip of his tongue between his teeth, and only looked at Martha once before handing over his gift, a paper bag containing a dozen yams. "They're from my patch," he said, and looked away.

"Hate, hate," grated Lily and gave Patrick's ear a hard tweak. "Tell your brother how much you hate him, Patrick. Show him. Break his ribs. Yank his tongue out. Make him bleed!"

"Everything I say he says I'm dumb," shouted Patrick. "He's dumb!"

Lily made them fight. She stood over them, and every time there was a letup plowed in with her own fists and wasn't particular about where the blows fell. She received quite a few and rolled with them. She tasted dirt and heard her dress rip.

The end came, and she lay exhausted in the dirt. Patrick and Danny got to their feet, looked at her, looked at each other, and loped off to the tent.

Lily turned her face into the dirt and, though what she said to it made no sense to her, said it anyway. "Fight," she said. "Fight."

She had just named her future.

Six

Judson spent hours making a study of the hollow and drawing plans for a log house. Early on Sunday afternoon he showed the plans to Lily and Martha. Martha had always wanted a chandelier, so the sketch showed an elaborate drawing of one but did not call for any windows or doors.

Judson sunk his teeth into that one, and with his usual mental agility admitted that some of the plan's details were still in his head. "We can figure out later where we want the windows and doors. Right now the main thing is for me to get out there and get the logs cut so I can put up the walls and the roof."

Martha dared to ask, "How are you going to get the logs back here once you've cut them, Jud?"

"Why," said Judson, "the mules will bring them back. Tomorrow when I'm in Sweet Root seeing about the power for our electricity I'm going to buy

a pair of mules. I thought I told you that."

Martha sipped her breakfast drink. It was grain kind, and she wanted coffee, black and stron Lily wanted bacon and toast. Instead cottage chee and dried peaches stared at her from her plate.

Said Martha, "Jud, do you know how much mule cost? And do you know how much money we have now?"

For a second Judson was annoyed, but then his face cleared. "I'll shop around for the mules. If I have to, I'll use my credit."

"You don't have any credit," said Martha.

"Everybody's got credit," said Judson. "This whole country is built on it." For him there were no impossibles, only possibles. The sun was up, there was the splashing of water, the wind was fresh, and there, shining in the sun, was the ax, its blade newly whetted. Judson was eager for the trees that would creak and fall under the blows of his ax. He wanted to see the chips fly and, with the first toppling, stand off and bawl, "Timber!" the way it was done in those old romantic movies where the heroes were lumberjacks.

Judson picked up his ax and hollered for Danny, who came slinking from the tent. He didn't want to be the second in command and said so. "Why can't Lily be it? She's older than I am and a lot stronger. Why can't she go help you get the logs?"

Waite had brought a panful of raw chicken pieces. He looked at Martha and looked at her and called her "ma'am." "Ma'am, you get out your spider, roll these pieces up in a little flour mixed with salt and pepper, fry them till they're crisp on the outside, and you'll have some good eating."

"A spider," said Martha. "You're suggesting that I flavor this chicken with a spider? Oh no. I won't do that. I don't like spiders."

Charmed, Waite regarded Martha. "Ma'am, the kind of spider I'm talking about is an iron skillet."

"I have a skillet, but it's not iron," said Martha.

"Then I'll lend you mine," said Waite. "It's a necessity when you fry chicken. If you don't believe me, ask Doe here. His fried chicken never fails. He not only knows how to cook it but is an expert at raising it, too. There is a kind of sensitive side to his chicken raising, though. He makes pets of his chickens. He even gives them names. He gets so attached to them that when it comes their time to go, I'm the one who has to send them. Isn't that right, Doe?"

"It wasn't Elizabeth's turn," mourned Doe.

"See what I mean?" said Waite. "He's worse than a woman. It gets on my nerves sometimes, and if I wasn't so lazy I'd do something about it. I'd find somebody to marry and live in Sweet Root."

"Ha," said Doe. "You know you don't want to do

that. You know you can't forget that if it wasn't for me you wouldn't even be here. You know you can't forget about that time you had the measles and would have died if it hadn't been for me."

"Tell it again," said Waite.

"I was clerking in one of his daddy's stores," related Doe. "But when Waite took sick I was sent to help his mama. She put him and me in a rocker and we stayed there for three days and three nights. He wouldn't let anybody else hold him. I wasn't anything but a boy then myself." With quite a bit of relish and some huffiness Doe rattled this tale off, and then reminded Waite that home things needed doing. He made it plain that he wasn't crazy about lending the spider but said if Lily and Martha wanted to go with him and Waite to get it, he'd try to do without it for a day or two.

Patrick declared his loud intention to go along, and Martha said, "Go and let me have some rest from you." She didn't want to walk anywhere and didn't want Patrick's kiss. She didn't want the chicken either because it meant messy work, but put the pieces in a jar and carried it to the Falls.

Out on the trail, Patrick skipped ahead of the others. He pulled up short to see a deer bound from a thicket. The trace was narrow and rutted, just wide enough to accommodate one vehicle. There were patches of swampy ground and then higher ground. Pokeweeds showed their red stems.

All of this was Snow property, and Lily listened to the sound of her father's ax ringing in the distance. Somewhere between South Dakota and Florida she had abandoned the habit of rope-leashing Patrick to her waist, and now, all in a second, he left the trail and sped away from her, running toward the sound of the ax, and crying, "Papa! Papa!" Trees and bush growth were in the way, but none of it stopped Patrick.

Disgusted with him and with herself, Lily hiked her skirt so that it cleared her knees and charged after him. Several times she lost sight of him as he zigzagged through the trees. Thorns snagged at her. She fought her way out of a brush tangle. The forest was dark and then light again.

The sound of the ax had stopped. It had stopped because Judson had collapsed. Beside his fallen tree he lay on the ground.

There was quiet and there was commotion. Danny ran up to Lily. "He just fell over, Lily! What's the matter with him? He just fell over!"

Patrick was pawing at Judson, stroking his face and wailing, "Papa! Are you sick, Papa?"

There were Waite and Doe, who had come up behind Lily. Waite knelt beside the still figure. He put his ear to Judson's chest and slapped the pale face. "Judson, wake up. Judson, open your eyes."

Judson's eyelids fluttered. He lifted an arm and let it fall.

"Probably it's the change of climate," suggested Doe.

Lily stared down at her father. "No. It's something left over from when he was a boy." She didn't want to touch her father. She only wanted this scene to go away. A thought struck her—that her father could die, if not this time, then the next or the next.

Her father had his eyes open, and Waite, with an arm under him, was saying, "Take it easy, Judson. It's all right now."

Lily took in a breath and took in another. All of the faults she had found with him, all of the things she had not said to him or done for him rushed at her. Her next words and the harsh way in which she spoke them shocked her. "No. It is not all right. He is sick, and he has got to go to a doctor. I don't care what he says, he has got to go. Now."

Her father's protest was unsteady. "I am not sick."

"You are," asserted Lily. And ruthlessly said, "You could die. Do you want to die? If you die, Mama will be a widow."

Judson's eyes rested on Lily's face. He glared at her, and she glared back. He weakened. "I don't have any money for a doctor. Doctors charge money."

Waite put a hand on Judson's shoulder. "Friend, let me take you to a doctor. There isn't one in Sweet Root, but there's a good one at Gillan Court, twenty-five miles down the road from here. He got over being in a hurry for his money a long time ago."

So that was the way the scene was made to end. Doe hustled off to get Waite's pickup, the two men put Judson in it, and away they went, Judson looking wan and defeated. He had some last-minute worried words for Lily. "Don't tell your mother about this, and don't let your brothers tell her. Tell her I've gone with Waite and Doe to look at mules. And don't leave my ax out here. I'll be back in time for supper."

He wasn't, and Martha didn't believe the mule story. She was canny and pried the scared truth from Danny and Patrick. When it was out, she sent them to the tent, took a lantern, and went to the Falls, leaving Lily to clear away the remains of supper, to stoke the fire glowing on its rocks, to wait and listen, to listen and wait.

In the tent, Danny and Patrick slept or pretended to sleep. From the darkness came the hooting of owls. One could laugh.

Out of the darkness came Waite and Doe. Waite was first out of the pickup. At once he told Lily that the doctor in Gillan Court had put her father in the little hospital there. "So he can be watched for a couple of days," he said, and asked for Martha. Down by the Falls the light from her lantern was moving back and forth and in a circle. Waite went to it and it stopped.

Standing straight in the light from the camp lantern and that from the fire, Lily turned her back on the Falls. Doe was watching her, and she snapped at him. "You're glad for all of this trouble, aren't you? Why? Is it because now you think we won't stay? So you and Waite Cody can keep it all to yourselves?"

"This is no place for a sick man and his family," declared Doe.

"Maybe not," said Lily. "But at least a piece of it is ours."

"It will fight you," said Doe.

"We will fight back," retorted Lily. She said that then only to heckle Doe because she disliked him, but when she and her mother were left alone and they talked, the idea appeared as more than just four quick words.

Martha wept into her handkerchief. "I wish I had never heard of this place. I wish we hadn't come. I have never felt so alone or been so confused."

"You are not alone, Mama," said Lily. She wanted to grab her mother and shake her. She spooned Postum into a cup, added hot water, and handed the cup to her mother.

Martha didn't want Postum. She poured it out onto the ground, moving her feet to avoid the trickle. "Tomorrow morning I'll have to go to Gillan Court and see about your father. I'll have to talk to the doctor about him. After that we'll probably know

96

what we are going to do. Mr. Cody thinks we should move into Sweet Root. He knows of a house and a small store that are for rent. He thinks there is room in Sweet Root for a small grocery. Your father could do that again."

"Papa wants what's out here," said Lily.

Martha stalked to the door of the tent and came flouncing back. "Lily, we have to give this up. There can't be a house for us out here. There can't be anything for us out here because your father won't be able to make anything of it. Mr. Cody talked with the doctor a little, and that was the verdict. Your father's heart is not right, and he has got to learn to pace himself. A grocery store won't kill him. Building a house and farming peanuts might, though." Martha's tears were finished. She was finished with the day. On the way back to the tent she picked up a rock and hurled it in the direction of the Falls. The lantern in her hand lighted the tent only for several minutes.

Alone by the fire, Lily watched the light in the tent go out. So we are right back where we started, she thought. Again the rented house and again the little grocery store. And the junk. There will be junk again all piled in a corner. Danny will deliver the groceries. He'll have a secondhand bicycle and will be told that he isn't to use the front doors when he makes his deliveries. And after a while Patrick will be old enough for a bicycle, and then he'll find out about back doors and front doors. Papa will pretend he loves selling groceries. The ladies will come to his store and squeeze the bread, and they'll hate Mama because she'll hate them first. Papa won't hate anybody. He might go off somewhere and cry, but then he'll come back and say his eyes are red because he ran into a dust storm. He'll sell this land for whatever he can get for it and dribble the money away. My God, my God, is there never going to be anything better for us?

The laughing owl had moved up closer to the campsite, and Lily walked over to where, earlier in the day, she had left her father's ax. With both hands she lifted it. Its weight surprised her. The idea floundering in her head surprised her. A couple of times it drowned but surfaced again and again, and presently did not appear as a waste.

Lily took a grip on the ax handle and walked out a way. The moon was yellow, and by its amber light Lily regarded the trunk of a tree. She took up a spraddle-legged stance, lifted the ax, and took a swing at the tree's trunk. The ax and the tree trunk connected, and the impact sent her staggering backward. In a rage, she sprang forward and swung again. There was a crack, and some slivers of bark flew out. Slivers were all that they were.

Lily returned to the camp. In the tent she lay in

her sleeping bag staring into the blackness. On the opposite side of the tent Martha slept.

Patrick came out of his bag and crept to Lily. He whispered that he needed a drink of water, and she took him outside to the bucket and the dipper. He drank and wiped his wet mouth with the back of his hand. "Mama said Papa is sick."

"Only a little," said Lily.

"She said he can't chop down any more trees. Can he?"

"No."

"Then we can't have our log house, can we?"

"No," said Lily. She meant yes. The house that would eventually stand in the hollow at the Falls wouldn't be a mansion, of course, but it would be safe and it would look right. She would be able to ride away from it without worry for those she would leave behind. When she was old she would be able to open an album with a pasted picture of it on one of its paper leaves and say, "That's the house I built for my family when I was a girl. Until I was married I lived in it with them. That room there on the corner was mine. That's when we lived in the hollow."

On his unseen perch just beyond the tent's rear wall the roaming owl screamed his laughter.

Seven

On Tuesday Martha brought Judson home, and on
Wednesday the Snows packed up and left the Falls.
In Sweet Root, on the steps of the house for rent,
Waite Cody and the owner were waiting. A keen
wind was blowing, and it lifted the dirt in the bare
yard. The house was frame with a tin roof. Its floors
sloped, but its owner pointed out that it came fur-
nished.

Lily thought that the house owner must be a fe-
male striver. She wore trousers held up by a man's
broad belt and had a stern haircut. She said that
everybody in Sweet Root called her Miss Priscilla.
She and Waite swapped wisecracks in the way friends
do. When she mistook Martha for Judson's daughter, Waite clapped her on her shoulder and laughed.
She said she knew that the house needed some re-
pair, but if the Snows were smart they'd take it
anyway because rental properties in Sweet Root were
scarcer than hens' teeth. "When they fall down or

burn down, they stay that way," she said. "Look on some of the back streets and you'll see what's left of them. Nobody cares."

Danny said, "Hens don't have teeth."

"Honey," said Miss Priscilla, "that's what I mean." She owned the store for rent, too, and Waite went with her and Judson to look at it.

Full of ideas, Judson came back alone. "After I get the place cleaned up and painted, I'm going to scout around for a couple of little tables and some chairs so the ladies who buy from me will have a place to sit and enjoy a cup of free tea after they've done their shopping. Ladies like to be served tea in pretty little cups. It makes them feel pampered. If I pamper them, they'll buy from me."

"We don't have any pretty little cups," said Martha. "Only big ugly ones."

Judson hugged her. "You leave the store to me. I know what I'm doing."

Lily could not look at her father. "What are you going to do about the land at the Falls?"

"Nothing" was the answer. "It isn't worth anything except to somebody who could build on it, and I could look a month of Sundays and never find anybody around here like that. I've found that out. So we'll just forget about it for a while. It isn't going anyplace. In the summer it will be a place where we can picnic and swim."

Judson stood in the doorway watching Martha and

the boys, who had gone out into the yard. The street running past it was unpaved. If it had a name, it wasn't advertised.

Sweet Root's school was several country blocks away, and on Monday Lily and Danny joined its student ranks. Mrs. Reed asked Lily if she wouldn't like to take the school's course in home economics.

"I took it last year," said Lily. "I tried to learn how to sew but couldn't. I sewed the hem of a skirt shut. Twice."

"Then you'd better take it again," said Mrs. Reed. "I will put you down for it. You will like the girls in that class. You will like the girls in all of your classes."

Lily didn't like them. They were so priggish, so without style, so Sweet Rootish. They looked at Lily's legs and watched the way she walked, and looked away.

The boys in Lily's classes looked her over, and she looked back. Such babies they were with their pink cheeks and their white teeth sticking out. They were wide-shouldered and thick-chested. None looked underfed.

In Lily's estimation, Silent Joe Murphy was Sweet Root's dunderhead. He was never without an arm-load of books, but when he was asked to recite, about all that came out of him was "Oh, ummmmm," or "Ah, ummmmm." It appeared that he had a fondness for bananas. Every day he came to school with a pair of fresh ones poking from his pockets.

Lily, too, liked bananas and had never thought that her taste for them had anything to do with her ancestors. She believed that humans had always been humans, yet when she observed Silent Joe plowing down the hallways of the school, she thought of apes.

On his way to or from some personal mystery, Silent Joe frequently passed the house on no-name street either walking or chugging by in his truck. When he walked, he carried a long box by its handle.

In the evenings Lily took Patrick for walks, and sometimes they passed Bragg's service station. If Billy was sitting in his glassed-in office, he'd jump up, rush to the door, and wave. If he was outside servicing a car and looked up from what he was doing, he'd make mistakes. He'd drop something or slop something, and his annoyed customer would grumble things that were not compliments in a loud voice.

One evening Billy's pet duck came flapping around from in back of the station and ran after Lily and Patrick, nipping at the backs of their legs.

"Oh, he's cute," cried Patrick, and tried to hug the duck, but it didn't want to be hugged.

Lily picked the bird up and, followed by Patrick, carried it into Billy's station.

Billy had newspaper spread out on the floor and

was working on an old table. Wads of steel wool and sheets of sandpaper littered the paper. "It's for my mother," said Billy. "She wants it refinished." He didn't know what to do with his hands or feet. He stood and fastened his eyes on Lily.

"Here's your bird," said Lily, and handed it over.

Billy set the duck on the floor. "He wants a ginger snap," he said, and punched the no-sale key to the cash register. Its drawer flew open. Billy pulled three ginger snaps from a paper bag, banged the drawer shut, knelt, and offered the cookies to the duck. "Here, Ethel."

The duck made ravenous noises, gobbled the cookies, and waddled out.

Patrick would have gone with it, but Lily held on to him. "It's almost dark," she said, "and we've got to go home. If we aren't there pretty soon, they'll think we're lost."

"I'm not lost," said Patrick. "I know where I am." The inside and outside lights of the station were on. Patrick went over to the table. "It's ugly but it's nice."

"It will be nicer when I get through with it," rattled Billy. All a-rattle, he looked around for chairs. There were two, and he dragged them to the table. "I can't close up till nine o'clock. I have to keep the station open every night till nine o'clock, but if you wanted to stay here with me, we could play a game.

I play checkers with my mother. Do you like checkers?"

"They're not my game," said Lily, and she and Patrick went home. Waite Cody was there in the living room talking with Martha. They were drinking real coffee.

Waite came often to the house. He took a wrench to the Snows' faulty plumbing system, and climbed up onto the roof to nail down a corner of tin that flapped in the wind. He brought bags of choice, fresh fruits such as the Snows couldn't afford even at wholesale prices. It was Waite who arranged for Judson to borrow money from Sweet Root's bank. Because it drank gas, Judson parked the Chevrolet in the Snows' backyard and walked to and from his store.

In Waite Cody, Lily saw a touch of greatness. He was a man who could afford to live anywhere and be anything, yet the Snows' kitchen was good enough for him. None of their troubles were too big or too small for his attentions. When he smiled at Lily and called her "Girl Thing," she was made freshly aware that she was young and desirable.

One chilly evening Lily sat on the steps of the front porch with Waite, and they talked for an hour. When he left, she couldn't remember what they had talked about. She stood and looked out into Sweet Root's night world.

It was too dark to make anything of the vague shape standing at the far edge of the sandy lot on the opposite side of the street. Anyway, Lily knew what it was: a house partially gutted by a long-ago fire and now abandoned. It was one of those houses Miss Priscilla had described. Nobody cared about it except Patrick, who, on a glum afternoon, said, "The people that lived in it might have left some pretty little cups like Papa needs for the tea ladies."

"They didn't leave any pretty little cups," said Lily. "I went over there and looked."

"The fire made the chimney fall down on their dog, and it's still there," said Patrick.

"There is no dog in that house," said Lily.

"Some gold money, then," said Patrick. Arguing with him was like arguing with a dictionary. Lily took him to the house and showed him that there was no dog, there were no pretty little cups, and there was no gold money. There was rubble, and in what had been a living room there was Silent Joe Murphy sitting beside his long box. He was gazing at the walls and eating a banana. The box was open, and Lily saw that it held a carpenter's tools.

"Oh," cried Patrick. "You came back for your dog. Where is he?"

"Oh, ummmmm," said Silent Joe.

"He thinks that the people who lived here had a dog and went off and left it," explained Lily.

Silent Joe deliberated this weighty question. "Ah, ummmmm, no dog."

Patrick forgot the dog and transferred his interest to Silent Joe. "What're you sitting here for?"

"For a while," answered Silent Joe.

With his eyes Patrick examined Silent Joe's face. "Does this house belong to you?"

"Kind of," said Silent Joe.

"Kind of what?"

"My father said I could have it if I wanted it."

"Don't he want it?"

"No."

"Why?"

"Because houses aren't his business. He owns trucks. A whole fleet of them. They're his business. He likes to make money, and this house won't make him any."

"Why don't you fix it?"

"I've been thinking about it," said Silent Joe. "But after I got it fixed, nobody would want to live in it. People want brick houses. They don't want wooden ones anymore."

"I like wood ones," said Patrick. "The windows to this one didn't burn up, did they?"

"No," said Silent Joe. "Neither did the doors. A lot of it didn't burn up."

"My dad is going to have a grocery store like the one we had in South Dakota," said Patrick. "When you need some cheese or some pickles, you go buy it from him. He'll give you a cup of free tea in a pretty little cup." He patted Joe's hand and skipped away to first one doorway and then another.

"Who is he?" said Silent Joe.

"He's my brother," said Lily. At that time she did not see Silent Joe as the important person he was to become to her. It was days before she went again across the sandy lot to the burned-out house.

The Snows had then been in the house on no-name street a little over a week. Two women had come to call on Martha. To hide its dirt and fray, Martha had covered the living room couch with towels, tacking them into place.

The women sat on the couch and said that the towels were a clever idea. They said wasn't the hired help situation in Sweet Root something, though? That it was almost impossible to find anybody who wanted to work no matter how much you paid them. They said they paid their hired girls more than they could make anywhere else, but still they only showed up about half of the time. They wanted to know if Martha had ever considered doing outside work. When they left, Martha snatched the towels from the couch and hurled them into the washing machine standing on the back porch.

In his store, Judson painted shelves and walls with slow strokes. His heart wasn't always willing to do what his arms wanted to do, and then he would have to sit and wait for the shaky moment to pass. During after-school hours Danny came to smear paint and wash flyspecked windows.

When Judson looked at Danny, he had to check his sighs. The boy wasn't really interested in the store, wasn't interested in anything, lived too much inside himself, and wouldn't talk about what was there.

Judson released one of his sighs and glanced at the mess Danny had made of one of his shelves. The mess could be corrected, it wasn't important. The kid who had made it was. The kid, thought Judson, needs something. A boy place. Some place where he can run and be a little wild and crazy like boys are supposed to be. And he needs to know that it's his, that he won't have to leave it next week, next month, or next year. But I can't give him that. This is all I can give him.

Judson felt like bawling. Instead he dipped his brush again and put a grin into his voice. "If we aren't careful, we'll have the best-looking place of business in Sweet Root by the time we get all of this done."

Danny threw his soapy rag into his bucket. "Lily should be here helping us. She's not crippled. But you know where she is right now?"

"There's no telling," said Judson.

"Out chasing around the way she always does," said Danny.

He was mistaken. Lily was not out chasing around. She was sitting in the burned-out shell that was Silent Joe's house having an earnest conversation with him.

Said Lily, "I know where there's a house you could fix, and afterward people would want to live in it."

"Where?" said Joe.

"At Sweet Root Falls," said Lily.

"What's wrong with it?" asked Silent Joe.

"It isn't built yet," said Lily.

"If it isn't built yet, then it isn't a house," said Joe.

"It will be as soon as I decide who is going to help me build it," said Lily.

"Ahhhh," said Silent Joe, and looked at Lily as if she had turned into a first-class miracle. He was her first-class miracle, and on the way to school the next morning she told Danny that she was going riding with him that afternoon. "He's got a nifty little truck, and this afternoon I get to take a ride in it."

"Joe Murphy," said Danny. "Is that the best you can do? If you like men so much, why don't you get one? Why don't you get Billy Bragg?"

"Billy Bragg doesn't have time to do the things I want to do," said Lily. "He has to stay in his station and run it."

"Or Waite Cody," said Danny, goading her. "He's probably about as old as Papa, but that's all right. He's a man."

"I never know where to find Waite Cody," said Lily. "So see? Man-crazy like I am, I'm stuck with Joe Murphy."

"You're crummy," said Danny and, breaking away from her, raced to the school ground. Its red swings and slides were alive with young children. Older students stood about in boy groups and girl groups waiting for the morning's first bell. The girls put their curly heads together and talked about clothes and movie heroes.

In Sweet Root there was no other kind and no demand for them. Sweet Root's young male population knew this and itched with knowing it. They wanted to go out and conquer something, carve their names in something, suffer for something, even die for something. They wanted something of their own, a cause, a secret union. But what they wanted had to sleep, had to be put away for a while. Maybe for a while, maybe forever. For there were tall fathers in Sweet Root, and they knew what they wanted of their tall sons.

So the sons sat in classrooms poring over algebra problems and learning about Augustus Caesar. Several of these sons drove light, open-bodied trucks to school. Beside them Silent Joe's appeared as a piece that had been hauled up out of a brackish pond. One of its fenders was gone, it was stained, it coughed and had a bad case of the trembles. It was not very faithful to Joe. There were times when he had to get out, push it to a curbing, and walk. On the way to the Falls that afternoon it straightened up and behaved.

It was the kind of day that old persons and sick ones notice. Blue with the crisp blueness of fall, it spoke of things finished and of things to come. At the Falls the squirrels looked down from piney branches and scolded Lily and Silent Joe.

Joe made several trips around the house foundation, bending to scratch its surface with a nail. He asked questions, laid Judson's plans out to examine them, and looked up and out to study the lay of the land. "The road is level, and that will make the skidding job easier on both us and the mules. What about the mules?"

"I haven't been to see the mule man yet," said Lily. He would not, she was certain, be an easy one to deal with, and she was not yet sure how she would go about this, so she was stalling. "I'll go see him tomorrow," she promised.

Silent Joe wanted tomorrow but didn't want to waste today. He brought a yellow hard hat from his truck, set it on his head, brought out an ax, trotted out to the nearest grove of pines, and with six blows brought down two young slender trees.

"Those aren't logs," said Lily.

"As soon as I strip them and make crotches in their ends to hold the logs they'll be our lifting poles," said Joe. "Lifting poles are what you use to raise a log wall."

"I see," said Lily. She didn't. She saw the two leafy saplings only as they were. She saw the land, and its distance and breadth made her want to laugh. It was shaggy. It was rough and needed some taming. It was Snow. The house that would stand on it would be Snow.

Doe was pensive when he talked with her about the house that day. He came out of his end of the woods and stood before her, whacking at everything in sight with his walking stick. He looked at the raw place where the saplings had been and said, "I saw you and Silent Joe when you drove in. Where is Silent now?"

"He's gone back to the Falls," said Lily.

"What are you and him up to?"

"That is a private matter," said Lily.

Doe threw his stick away, sat on the ground, and offered a dour compliment. "You're almost as pretty as your mama."

"Thank you," said Lily.

"I wish you could like me," said Doe. His wrinkles were gentle, and his eyes were honest.

Lily gave in to the honesty in his eyes. "I like you."

Doe tried burying his chin in his collar. It would

not stay buried and he gave up on it. "You seen Waite lately?"

"He had supper with us last evening," said Lily. She did not say that Waite had cooked it—fried chicken and Cody gravy.

"He's left me and is living at the hotel in Sweet Root," complained Doe. "Took my spider with him. I don't care about him leaving me, you understand. He likes the company of girls and gets lonesome for them. But wouldn't you say that him taking my spider with him was an insult?"

"I would say that's insulting," said Lily.

"He knows my spider was my main cooking piece, and he knows I won't get to town to buy me another one. I never go to town. He knows that, but he still sallied off with my spider. When you get back to Sweet Root, do me a favor. Find Waite and tell him I want my spider. You and Silent Joe can bring it when you come tomorrow."

"I didn't hear myself say we were coming again tomorrow," said Lily.

Doe went after his stick and came back with it to sit again. His eyes picked Lily clean. "You and Joe are fixing to put up a house out here, aren't you?"

"Yes," said Lily.

"Does your papa know it?"

"No."

"Does your mama?"

"No. It's going to be a surprise."

114

"Is it going to be a log house?"

"Yes."

"Logging can be dangerous work. It's not for children."

"We're not children."

"Well," commented Doe, "Silent knows about how to engineer a house. His daddy don't want him to listen to it, but that's his calling. When Waite and I were putting our place up, Joe was our helper. He wrote down everything we did. You going to use a tractor or mules to help with your skidding?"

"Mules," said Lily.

"Joe is a good teamster," said Doe.

"He is going to be my teamster," said Lily.

"Skidding is where you drag the logs from the stumps to the place where you're going to store them or work on them or whatever you're going to do with them," said Doe. His smile was toothless. "Don't let Silent talk your head off," he added, and cackled in the way an old lonesome man does who hasn't much left to be funny about.

Doe knew Silent Joe well enough to joke about his conversation habits. Lily knew him better. She knew that now on dusky street corners and in furtive alleyways he could be seen huddled with a twosome or a foursome, and he was talking, talking.

The tall sons of Sweet Root were listening, listening.

Eight

Lily went to see the mule man. The lettering on his shop window didn't say he was a dealer in mules. It said that he was a jeweler and watchmaker. He stood behind one of his glass showcases peering at Lily, and every second or so put his loupe back in his right eye and bent again to peer at the little pile of Lily's getaway jewelry spread out on a square of purple velvet. "The little football is only gold-plated," he said. "But I might give you ten dollars for it."

"It's been in my mother's family for a hundred years," murmured Lily. "Probably when they got starved out of Ireland one of them brought it with him."

The mule man alias jeweler gave the football another examination. "All right, I'll give you fifteen for it, but that's as high as I'll go. I don't get much call for gold-plated footballs."

"What about the other stuff?" asked Lily.

"Mostly slum," said the jeweler.

"Even the ring with the pearls?" said Lily. It was useless to bat her eyelashes or try to draw attention to her legs. The mule man–jeweler was paunchy, and it had been a long time since he had had to do anything to his head except pass a wet washrag over it. It was a pale knob and there wasn't a hair on it. He had avoided showing any interest in the pearl-studded ring but now with tender fingers lifted it from the tufted mat. "It's a nice piece. You shouldn't sell it. It's something to keep."

Lily met the jeweler's gaze. Was he a father? Sure he was. He was a husband and a father. He had a daughter and had promised both her and her boy-friend a shotgun wedding if ever he caught them at anything more serious than sharing the same hymn-book.

Said Lily, "I don't want that ring anymore. When I look at it I don't feel decent, and I am. The man who gave it to me thought I'd jump into a pile of hay with him, but I didn't. I want to sell the ring."

The jeweler's gaze had deepened. He switched it from Lily back to the ring. "You wait here. I want to take this number to my private room and give it a special look-see." He was gone fifteen minutes. When he returned to the front of the shop, he told Lily that the green stone in her ring was good jade and that the pearls were natural, not cultured.

"I'd like to have been the guy who dived for those pearls and brought them up," he said. "When I was a young man I wanted to run off and sign on with one of those ships that goes out to hunt for treasure."

"Why didn't you go?" said Lily.

"I wasn't let," said the jeweler. "My dad wanted me to be like him, so I stayed home and got to be like him."

"I know how to swim, but I don't know how to dive," said Lily.

"I wasn't just talking about diving," said the jeweler, becoming a little testy. "I was talking about getting on a boat and steaming to the other side of the world. But it's understandable if you don't understand me. Adventure talk is a different language, and nobody speaks it anymore."

"Will you buy the ring?" asked Lily.

"You would want too much for it," replied the jeweler.

"I'll sell it to you for a fair price if you'll rent me two of your mules for a fair price," said Lily.

The jeweler blinked. "What?"

"I'll need them for a week or two," said Lily. She knew that she had caught the jeweler's interest but wondered how far she dared to go with him, how much to tell and how much to hold back. He was winding the watch on his wrist but was studying her. After a little he said, "Mules are valuable animals."

Father's Day or Christmas present. She gave such things as jackknives and magazine subscriptions. Everything had to be bought.

The jeweler thought of his father, and to his memory said, "Old man, I don't care what you would have done. I did what I wanted to do, and it's right, it's right."

The jeweler pulled his night shades and went to his back room to collect the lunch he had not eaten at noon, while down Sweet Root's central street Lily walked with quick, confident steps. She passed the hotel and didn't look in its direction. The store that sold hard hats was already closed.

Lily bought her hat and boots the next afternoon at the outfitter's store in Gillan Court. The woman who took her money asked Silent Joe how he had been but brushed his answer aside. She showed Lily a hat with a metal crown such as construction workers wear. "Pink isn't your color," she said, "and it's too big for your head, but it's the only one I've got left. I had a run on these yesterday. A bunch of boys cleaned me out. They was having themselves a grand time, laughing and whooping it up. I didn't ask them what it was all about."

To pay for the hat and boots, Lily had to remove her shoe and peel back its lining. The woman behind the counter made no comment, but on the way back to Sweet Root, Joe said, "You shouldn't carry that money around with you."

Lily turned and looked out through the shop's window at the dying afternoon. Red sun stained the western sky, and in its light the town of Sweet Root lay stale and quiet.

Still wondering whether to trust him, Lily faced the jeweler. "Sweet Root is dead."

The jeweler agreed. "Yep. It's just waiting for somebody to come along and cover it up. And cover them up."

"Who is them?" inquired Lily.

"Them are the ones who make the rules," answered the jeweler and shrugged.

Lily made a decision. She would have to either trust the mule man—jeweler or go elsewhere to look for mules to rent, and in Sweet Root there was no elsewhere. "Them don't make my rules," she said. "I make my own." Standing on the opposite side of the showcase, she put her elbows on it, put her face in her hands, and began to tell the jeweler about the log house she intended to build and about how Silent Joe and some of the others were going to help.

The jeweler stopped being a tired shopkeeper waiting for his watch to tell him it was time to go home to his supper, his slippers, and his newspaper. Several times he exclaimed, "Oh no. You can't. You can't keep a thing like that quiet in a little burg like this. They'll find out." But he didn't believe what he said. He was loving the conspiracy. He took steps backward and forward. He put a hand in his pocket and made some coins jingle. He started to laugh and changed his mind. Some pink color came into his cheeks, and his eyes brightened. He changed his mind again about the laugh. It came.

So a bargain was struck, and Lily tucked a little sheaf of currency into her shoe.

"But I don't want anybody but Joe to handle the mules," said the jeweler. "He knows how, and he knows how to take care of them."

Lily felt that she should reward the jeweler with more than her thanks and made him a promise. "When I find out who I'm going to marry, I'll make sure he buys my ring from you. I want a circle of diamonds."

The jeweler was affectionately amused. "If you're going to look for a husband in Sweet Root, you might be fresh out of luck. All the men here are either taken or too young to have enough money to buy you a circle of diamonds. There's Waite Cody, of course. He's living at the hotel now, and I see that he's taken to shaving every day and keeping his boots shined. He might be in the wife market, but if he is, I doubt he'd be looking for a child bride."

Lily did not want to discuss Waite Cody. She liked the way he looked at her when he came to the house, and liked the way he called her Girl Thing. But she didn't want to think about him much and didn't want

to talk about him at all. "We will take care of your mules," she told the jeweler.

The mule man–jeweler escorted her to the door of his shop. "You had better get you a hard hat, one like Silent Joe's. And some boots. When you're logging, trees have got a way of falling in the wrong direction. There's a store in the next block down the street that sells boots and hard hats, but if I were you I'd go to the outfitter's store in Gillan Court and buy them. The woman who runs it thinks curiosity is a sin, so she won't ask any questions."

The jeweler closed and locked his door behind Lily. He started to draw the night shades as was his custom, but put off doing it for a minute or two. Instead he stood looking out at the town, the dying town, and thinking about the ship he had never sailed on and thinking about his daughter. It was too late for the ship, and he couldn't stand his daughter. She was married now and had kids of her own but still thought that a mop was something somebody else should hang out on a line to dry. The way she whined about what she should have and what she didn't have gave him hives. He could count on having an attack of them every time he was dragged off to one of her heavy Sunday dinners. Not even a starving back-door moocher should have to endure one of his daughter's dinners and the talk that went with them. Daughter had never heard of making a

"It's safe," said Lily. And asked, "When will you go after the mules and take them to the Falls?"

"Today before dark," answered Silent Joe. "I'll take Doe's spider to him if you want me to and get him to say the mules are for him if anybody asks." Because it was needed for the mule rental and for materials that couldn't be salvaged from his burned-out house, he still fretted over the money, so on Saturday, when she went with him to the Falls, Lily had it in a lidded can and buried it.

As she was smoothing the last spadeful of earth back into place, a little army of booted lionhearts in hard hats came. It was early morning, and the hollow wasn't yet fully awake.

The lionhearts came in trucks. "We told everybody we were going on a field trip. We told them that we suddenly got this big urge to find out what nature is all about and we're going to study it till we do," they said, and laughed at this piece of mischief. Prepared to convert trees into logs, they had brought axes and saws. Prepared to skid logs from woodlots to the construction site, they slung down logging chains and cables. Acting sappy, they kissed the mules and told them how much they loved them. They were child-hearted but they were men, and when Silent Joe said it was time to work they settled down to it.

They called Lily "Boss Lady," so it was this:

"Boss Lady, what do you think you're doing?"

"I'm helping you clean out these bushes and other stuff in here so we can get to the trees," grunted Lily, shouldering a dead branch. It was heavy, and one of its sharp twigs raked her cheek. Even stuffed with newspaper, her hat kept slipping down on to her forehead, and she kept pushing it back. The stand of pines in front of her stood motionless. There was no wind that day.

From one of the pines a voice sang out. "Boss Lady, what do you think about this here tree?"

Lily stumbled over a gnarled ground creeper. The branch on her shoulder swung around, and for a second she was lost in its brittle foliage. Overhead and underfoot, the tough creepers were every-where, and everything stung or stuck. Roots that should have been willing to let go wouldn't let go. Everything was gritty. Everything was fighting her, even the dead branch.

Through the dried leaves of her branch, Lily saw one of the hard hats standing beside a tree. He was so fresh-faced, so sure of himself. She screamed at him, "What's there to think? It's a tree!"

"How big around you reckon it is?" called the hard hat.

"Ten inches! Twelve! Your eyes aren't painted on. Can't you see how big around it is?"

"I think it must be about twelve inches. You want it for one of your logs?"

"Yes!"

"You got a place picked out to run in case it falls the wrong way?"

"Yes!"

"Then stand back and watch this."

Lily took herself and her branch to a point of safety and from there watched the broad-shouldered ax man bring the pine down. It fell with a thud, and the ax man put his booted foot on it. His smile gleamed. He and the other lionhearts had found their cause.

With Silent Joe and Lily behind them, always right behind them or beside them, they streamed through the forest felling those trees where the ground was flat, avoiding those where it sloped, so that the cutting could be done from the ground.

Before the mules were brought up to drag the trees to the construction site, the trees first had to be made into logs, had to be trimmed of their branches and sawed into measured lengths. All of this, said Silent Joe, needed an expert. He said Doe was an expert logman, and he and Lily went after him.

So for the first time Lily saw the cabin snuggled in the upper end of the hollow. Except for the utility poles and wires strung out along the road, except for the road leading up to it and the chickens pecking at its wild lawns, its setting was true wilderness. Neat as any fussy woman would have had it, its log walls had been varnished and its windows were curtained.

Lily noticed the cabin's furniture and thought about the furniture she and her family didn't have. On the way back to the Falls she asked Doe if he knew how to make furniture out of logs. He said no, that that was one thing he had just never given no consideration to, that wood for furniture should be bought at a sawmill because it had to be dried first either by air or in a kiln. Drying by air, he said, could take two or three years.

Doe was all wound up. He said he was glad to help anybody out, help them build anything, so long as he wasn't treated like something that had just crept out from underneath a rock. He said he wasn't going to have no more of anybody treating him like he was their water boy. He said he hoped that the hotel in Sweet Root had bedbugs, and that he hoped a black panther would leap into the window of Waite Cody's hotel room and throttle some sense into him.

Nine

The work at the hollow caused paths to be worn across its grassy floor. Doe complained that all of the coming and going was tearing up the road and scaring the turtles. He complained more when the after-school crew showed up late.

Now in the work area up close to the house foundation there were big boxes containing bark that had been peeled from the logs. Doe insisted that the bark be kept dry so that it could be burned, so, to keep ground moisture from seeping in, the lionhearts set the boxes on stump stilts. Silent Joe brought tarpaulins to cover the boxes.

Up close to the house foundation there were also stacks of salvaged building materials. Using a chisel and hammer, Lily learned how to break brick away from mortar. By late daylight and by lamplight she and Silent Joe tore down the whole chimney in Joe's fire-damaged house. To the Falls went the bricks that would become the Snows' fireplace, and to the Falls went oak doors complete to butts, and windows complete to casings.

Lily told Doe that she thought she would take up cussing. He said, "Why would you want to do that?"

"So I could say something besides 'Oh fudge' when I drop a brick on my foot or hit myself with a hammer," reasoned Lily.

"Cussing is a bad habit," said Doe, and told her that cold water was the best remedy for bruises, and yellow kitchen soap the best remedy for soot-grimed hair and clothing. For work he gave her a pair of his old pants and one of his old shirts. He said he had been saving them for a rag rug he intended to make, but that there was plenty more where they came from.

On Lily, Doe's shirt was roomy, and she rolled its sleeves up. She tried the pants on and found that when she took two steps the pants took only one, so in her locked bedroom she cut them down to size and by hand restitched them. Her work clothes— the hat, boots, shirt, and pants—were a slight problem. Every day, before and after work time, she had to hide behind a tree to change her clothes.

Doe said a lady shouldn't have to do that, and he, Silent Joe, and the lionhearts stopped the work on the house long enough to build a log privy. It was placed well away from the Falls and downriver so that there would be no risk to either Doe's water supply or the Snows'.

"It shouldn't look like a privy," said Lily. "I want it to look like a little house but not too little. And I want it to have windows so it won't be dark inside."

Silent Joe said a privy was a privy, and Lily's didn't need windows.

But Doe said, "Oh, let's go for the gusto. If the lady wants windows, let's give her windows." So Lily got her windows.

Cooler weather had come. There was frost in the hollow one Saturday morning, and in Sweet Root mothers ran after their children to ask if undershirts had been remembered. Martha Snow yelled at some of the children who cut through her backyard, and an hour later they came streaking back to wipe their noses on the cold sheets blowing on her clothesline.

On another Saturday morning the first bottom logs to Lily's house in the hollow were set into place. Doe and Silent Joe had notched them at both ends so that they would lock at the corners.

Thinking of how the whole thing would look when it was finished, Lily blew her warm breath on her cold hands, and her heart beat a little faster. It was not yet winter then, not according to the calendar. But winter didn't care what the calendar said. It came early.

The day before Thanksgiving, Lily went home earlier than usual. The house was warm and quiet. Patrick was waiting for her and drew her into the kitchen to show her a twenty-pound, dressed turkey resting in a pan in the refrigerator. "Mr. Cody brought it. He's coming back tomorrow morning to bake it and help us eat it. He brought some real coffee, too, but they wouldn't let me have any."

"They didn't want you to have a caffeine attack," said Lily.

"Mama and Mr. Cody drank it all," said Patrick.

Lily sat down. There was a pain in her back, and her arms hurt. "Where is Mama now?"

Patrick rolled his eyes. "Gone with Mr. Cody."

"Did they say what time they'd be back?"

"No. They said they didn't know and for me to eat my sandwich and when you got home to tell you to take care of me."

"Where is Danny?"

"He had to go help Papa in his store, but he didn't want to. He was mad."

"One of these days I'm going to run my hand down Danny's throat and turn him wrong side out," said Lily. "Maybe that will make him glad."

"You going to take care of me?" said Patrick.

It was a trap question. "What do you need?" asked Lily.

Patrick looked around at the stove and the cabinets as if he expected them to tell him what he needed. He didn't know what he needed. He sat down and began to tell Lily of his troubles. "Nobody talks to me."

"I talk to you," said Lily.

Patrick ducked his chin. "No. Now you don't come home and I have to stay with Mama, and she don't talk to me. I look and look for you, but you don't come home. You never come home till dark and I wait and wait. Where do you go without me?"

As if I didn't have enough trouble without this, thought Lily. "I go with a friend," she said.

"I am your friend," declared Patrick.

Lily swallowed. "If you'll just let me sit here and rest for another minute, I'll take you to see Billy Bragg. You'll get to see his duck. You remember his duck?"

"Ethel!" cried Patrick. "Sure. Sure. He eats ginger snaps."

"Just give me a minute," pleaded Lily.

"Sure, sure," said Patrick. A minute was nothing to him. He had lots of them. He was starved for talk and wasn't particular about his subjects. He and Lily talked all the way to Billy's station.

Billy was sitting in his office reading a newspaper and gloomily watching for customers. He was chewing gum. His gloom left him when he saw Lily and Patrick coming through his door. In happy confusion he threw his wadded newspaper into a wastebasket and swallowed his gum.

"We came to see Ethel," shrieked Patrick. "Where is Ethel?"

With his eyes on Lily, Billy said, "Ethel? You came to see Ethel?"

"Patrick did," said Lily. "I came to see you."

Billy moved to the cash register and punched the no-sale key. Its drawer shot out, and from under the newspaper in the wastebasket Ethel appeared.

Patrick galloped to the bird and threw his arms around it. "Ethel! You were hiding in there, weren't you?"

Showing off to Lily, showing her that he knew how to be brotherly, Billy handed a bag of ginger snaps to Patrick. "Take Ethel over to that corner over there to feed him. It's warm there, and you and him can both have an eating good time. You want a chair? No, you don't need a chair. You can sit on the floor."

Lily sat in one of Billy's chairs. "Where is your mother's table? The one you were working on the last time we were here?"

"We took it home," said Billy. He didn't know whether to stand behind his chair or sit in it. He went to a cabinet and opened it. Three empty cans, a book, and an empty soft drink bottle fell out. Billy ignored the cans and bottle but lifted the book and stood holding it. "I was looking for something but forgot what it was."

"Did your mother like what you did to her table?" said Lily.

"The table," said Billy. "Oh yeah. Mama liked it. She ought to have. All that sanding and rubbing, all that waxing and oiling, near about killed me. It had about ten coats of old paint on it, and I had to strip all of it off to get to what was underneath. I had to haul it outside and then haul it back in again because some of the stuff you use to get old paint off isn't good for your lungs. I'll never jump on a job like that again, I can tell you. I'd rather eat my beans off the floor than do it again. I can still smell rottenstone. Smells like rotten eggs. And you see this book?" said Billy, thumping the book's cover. "I had to buy it and read the whole thing so I could do that table. Is it hot in here?"

"No," said Lily, "it's just right." Actually the station's office was a little too cool for comfort.

Billy was wearing a cold-weather cap; its ear flaps were turned up. He came toward her and thrust the book at her. "If you like books, you can have this one. I'm through with it. You want a Coca-Cola?"

"I don't like Coca-Cola," said Lily, accepting the book.

"Me neither," said Billy, eager to agree with her about anything. "I knew a guy in the Army that drank them for breakfast. His name was Swainheart, but you'd never have been able to tell it to watch how he acted. Every time he got around a girl he'd fall over his own feet."

Lily looked at Patrick and Ethel. Patrick was carefully dividing the last ginger snap, and Lily interrupted more about Swainheart and Billy's days in the Army to say that she and Patrick had to be getting along. The book was far more than she had come for, could have hoped for, and she was anxious to get home and read it. She had some trouble getting away from Billy. He followed her and Patrick out as far as the street's curbing and wistfully waved them off. The air was damp and gray.

On Thanksgiving Day, Judson kept his store open until noon but only one customer came in to buy a can of nutmeg. She didn't have time for a cup of tea, and Judson hurried out from behind his counter to open the door for her departure. He closed it quickly because the day was one for weather historians. It had rained the night before, and icicles hung from building eaves. The puddles in the streets were crusted over with ice.

Lily was in the store with her father, and he noticed what he hadn't been noticing for some time: that she had grown lanky as an overgrown boy, that she had become sloppy about the way she dressed and fixed her hair, that she had taken on the ap-

pearance of a little toughie. Her interest in his junk
was something new, too.

Judson spread fresh paper on a shelf and watched
Lily, who was wandering around looking at his collection of junk. His passion for junk was as strong
as ever. It had gotten a little out of hand. His present
collection of it had pieces that were big and clumsy
and couldn't be piled but had to be spread out.

With his thumbnail, Judson made a sharp crease
in his shelf paper, and continued to watch Lily. Why
should a girl who was almost a woman be so interested in junk? True, his own fondness for the
discards of others was something he couldn't shake,
couldn't get rid of. He didn't want to get rid of it.
Junk was a part of him. It was like his disease, only
there was no danger to it. He liked looking at it.
The sight of that old sideboard there, those old bed-
steads, that old secretary backed up against that far
wall, and those old painted chairs crouched around
that old painted table fed something in him. But a
kid like Lily didn't need that kind of food to keep
her going. From the looks of it she needed real food,
not the stuff dreams are made of.

Judson took a pound of butter from a food case
and wrapped it. "Real butter," he said to Lily. "When
we go home, we'll take it with us. It'll be good on
those potato rolls Waite said he was going to make
to go along with our turkey."

Lily put her hand in her jacket pocket and felt the wad of precious green bills there. "I think I know somebody who would take all of this furniture off your hands if you didn't want too much for it."

It didn't need weighing, but Judson set the pound of butter on his scale. Foolishly he had paid for the furniture and foolishly he had paid for its delivery. At the time he had thought it was the smart thing to do. He had thought that it would bring a quick profit, but his thoughts had been a mistake. Every other housewife in Sweet Root had some old furniture and didn't want any more.

Judson came to stand in front of the sideboard. Its thick coats of paint had made it hideous. Viewing it with a frank and now an unsentimental eye, Judson said, "It doesn't match anything. Nothing matches, but once I sell it I wouldn't want to take it back. Who is this somebody you're talking about?"

"You don't know her," said Lily. "She's a friend of Silent Joe Murphy's and lives way out from Sweet Root. She's blind."

"Oh, I don't think I'd care to sell this stuff to a blind person," said Judson. "It's junk."

"She needs it," insisted Lily. "And she wants it. I went with Joe to her house and described all of it to her, and she said she wants it. She gave me the money to pay for it but said I shouldn't let you bankrupt her."

"I would certainly not even try to bankrupt an old lady," said Judson, champion of old ladies.

"She is not old," said Lily. "She's younger than you are and isn't anybody you need to feel sorry for. She gets around."

"I couldn't deliver it," said Judson.

"Tomorrow or the next day Joe Murphy will come with his truck," said Lily. "I'll help him load it and we'll deliver it."

Her father began to have a good time. He did some excited figuring and, when he was satisfied with his figures, relieved Lily of everything in her pocket except its lining. "If your lady needs more, I know where I can get some real cheap."

"I'll tell her," said Lily, thinking of her bankroll in the buried can at the Falls. It had dwindled to the point of being something to begin worrying about.

But it was Thanksgiving, and worry could wait. Lily and her father closed the store and walked home. Lily carried the butter. In the Snows' kitchen Patrick stuffed two slices of it into a potato roll and blissfully watched it melt.

Martha was short with him. "Can't you wait until we are all at the table? Can't we be civilized just this once?"

"I am civilized," said Patrick.

Martha pushed him out of the way and carried the turkey into the dining room. Judson stood to carve it. Waite passed the plates up to him to be filled, one by one.

Patrick had some news. "Mr. Cody's got a new car."

Lily forgot about the pain that still nagged her back. She turned her head to look at Waite, who was sitting next to her. "Really? What kind?"

"It's blue," cried Patrick, and laughed as if blue were something to be laughed at.

"It's a Buick," said Waite.

"A Buick," said Judson. "I didn't see any Buick parked out in front. I didn't see anything parked out in front."

"Because it's not there," crowed Patrick. "Billy Bragg's got it."

"I only got it yesterday afternoon," explained Waite. "It needs servicing, so this morning I let Billy drop me off here and take it to his station. I'm to go after it about two o'clock."

Judson was happy for his friend, his good friend. He gave Waite a generous smile, went to look at his outside thermometer hanging from a nail on the front porch, and came back to report that the temperature still was below freezing.

At two o'clock the mud in the yard still stood up in frozen peaks, but Martha said she wanted a walk in the cold. Leaving the dishes and the kitchen clutter to Lily, she left the house with Waite. Saying he had had enough of cold air for one day, Judson stretched out on the living room couch and slept.

Patrick helped Lily with the dishes. Standing on a chair at the sink, he fished plates from the pan of rinse water and eyed each one before wiping it.

Lily tried to hurry him. "You don't have to look at every one before you wipe it. When I put them in that pan there, they're clean. Let's hurry so when Mr. Cody and Mama get back we'll be through with this. Maybe Mr. Cody will offer to take all of us for a ride in his new car."

Patrick held up a plate. "This one's got a little bone stuck to it."

"Wipe it anyway," said Lily.

With his dish towel, Patrick scraped at the bone. "All of us can't go for a ride in Mr. Cody's car. It's got too much stuff in it."

"Wipe the plate," said Lily.

Patrick wiped the plate. "Mr. Cody kissed Mama."

"Mr. Cody and Mama are friends," said Lily. "Mr. Cody and Papa are friends. Friends kiss each other."

"Danny was asleep, but I was looking out the window and I saw him do it. He put Mama's clothes in his car and covered them up with a blanket, and then he kissed her. You want me to show you how he did it?"

In the dishwater, Lily's hands were still. "Yes," she said.

"I can't reach you," said Patrick, still on his chair.

Lily withdrew her hands from her dishwater, turned, and leaned to receive Patrick's kiss. He set his lips on hers, and for a fraction of a second they clung. "Like that," he said, and picked up his wet towel. The little bone was floating in the rinse water, and the clock on the shelf said that it was three o'clock.

At ten minutes past three, Lily went to her mother's room. The bed in it had been made. Hanging from wire hangers there were clothes in the closet: bathrobes, some sweaters, some trousers, a raincoat with a torn sleeve, some house dresses. These were a man's clothes and a woman's, all mixed together. Martha's yellow dress and the blue one were missing. All of her good clothes were gone. The drawer that usually contained her manicure kit and her scarves was empty.

Lily took a shawl sweater from its hanger. It belonged to her father and, holding it, she went to the bed. She sat on its foot stroking the sweater and stroking the back of her neck because the pain in her back had moved up.

There was the sound of talk coming from the living room. Judson was awake and talking with Patrick, trying to argue him out of the notion of going to Billy Bragg's station to see what was keeping Mr. Cody and Mama. Patrick won the argument, and they went, and came back. Lily met them at the door.

Patrick was crying and Judson was trying to comfort him. "They've just taken the car out for a little spin, I told you. They're not lost. They haven't had an accident. Nothing's happened. They'll be here pretty soon. Go take your coat off and wash your face and hands. Lily will make us some cocoa."

Patrick would not be consoled. He didn't want cocoa. He threw himself at Lily. "Tell him about the clothes. I didn't. You do it."

"Clothes?" said Judson. "What clothes?"

Lily covered Patrick's ears with her hands, and dropped them. There was no use in trying to keep what had happened from him. He already knew.

Lily faced her father and told him about the clothes, the empty drawer, and the kiss.

At five o'clock her father didn't believe it. At nine o'clock his disbelief had begun to waver. At twelve o'clock midnight he stopped waiting for the police to come and tell him that there had been an accident. He stood at the open front door looking out into the frosty night. Before he closed the door for the last time that night he said, "I didn't tell her about selling the furniture. I should have told her."

Ten

On the Tuesday after Thanksgiving, Doe came to Sweet Root, came to the house on no-name street. Walked all the way, he said, and was Lily going to ask him in and give him something hot to drink or wasn't she?

Lily sat him down at the table in the kitchen and poured two cups of strong black coffee.

"Silent Joe and the others told me about your trouble," said Doe.

"It isn't going to kill us," said Lily.

"You look like you've been dragged through a knothole," remarked Doe.

Lily brought an opened can of evaporated milk from the refrigerator and slammed it down onto the table. "You'd better put some of this in your coffee. It's strong enough to get up and walk. Waite Cody brought it to Mama. I'll be glad when it's gone."

Doe fed milk into his coffee, poured some into

his saucer, blew on it, and drank. "I stopped to see your papa for a minute. Little Patrick was helping him serve tea to some ladies."

"He's hurting," said Lily. "So is Papa." She couldn't speak of her own hurt or that of Danny. Danny's was the silent kind. He went to school, went to help Judson in the grocery, and came home. He ate, and slept. He kept himself severely clean, and didn't fight with Patrick.

Lily's hurt was battle smoke. She had not allowed herself to cry or to look back and think of what might have been and couldn't be now. In deepest secrecy she had put what might have been away, put her teeth in her lip and turned her face to what was now. I've got my character, she thought. I've got my thoughts. I've got me.

She had friends. The day after Thanksgiving she and Silent Joe moved all of the secondhand furniture out of Judson's store, loaded it into Joe's truck, and took it to the Falls. The lionhearts followed her orders and set it in the privy. Nobody talked about what had happened. They didn't ask questions. They were friends.

Doe was a friend, and here he was now all twisted up with his hurt and upheaval but concealing it. "Yesterday," he reported, "we started making the shakes that are going to make the roof for your house at the Falls."

"I haven't quit you," said Lily. "Tomorrow right after school I'll be back."

Doe finished his coffee and set his cup in its saucer. "I thought you might be of a mind to leave school now."

"The law wouldn't let me do that, and I'm not a criminal, so I have to go," said Lily. "I've been out because of the way things are, but tomorrow I have to start back."

"Splitting them logs up to make shingles for your roof is not my idea of a play-party," said Doe. "But the boys are good at helping, and when we get them all nailed down into place you'll have a pretty roof. It ought to last you twenty or thirty years." He had seen what he had come to see and had heard what he had come to hear. Preparing to leave, he buttoned his coat. He stood, and there was one awful moment when Lily thought both he and she would break down, might even throw their arms around each other and howl. But then his stern smile came and so did hers, and solemnly they shook hands.

Almost every day Doe came to the privy at the Falls to sit in a cold corner and talk for a few minutes at a time during the hours Lily spent working there.

The privy had a plank floor, and its log walls had been chinked just as the walls of the log house would be chinked. Squatting in his corner, Doe said he didn't feel the cold.

Lily felt it. Her bones ached with feeling it. Because she worked with paint and varnish removers, rubbing oils, vinegar, and rottenstone, and because all were odious, she kept the privy windows wide open, and the cold that swept through the hollow blew in.

Working at restoring the sideboard, Lily lifted lengths of waxed paper from its top and saw that the paper had kept her paste-type paint remover from drying. The stripping action was completed. The old finish was wrinkled and soft. With the round edges of her putty knife, Lily slid the removal mass into a disposal can and with denatured alcohol cleaned the sideboard's surface. It satisfied something in the bottom of her to see the old wood mellowed to all shades of rich brown. When given two coats of varnish with much rubbing and hand sanding in between the coats, the old heavy piece glowed with its own particular brand of beauty.

"I did a good job on you," said Lily, and turned her attention to the four waiting chairs, the beds, and the table. There were stains, scars, dents, and scratches to be repaired. She made mistakes. Her hands grew blisters. She used muscles she didn't know she had, and they quivered. Time was her enemy. There was never enough of it. It was a race to beat her father, Patrick, and Danny home to the supper kitchen.

Danny had stopped complaining of her cooking. Whatever it was that had been snuffed out of him in his earlier years, whatever it was that had made him so surly, so always ready for an argument or a fight, was gone. His school grades improved. Judson bought him a secondhand bicycle so that again he could be a delivery boy, and he attached a red pennant to its wire basket. He said he didn't want anything for Christmas.

Christmas came, and on its eve Billy Bragg played Santa Claus to Patrick. When it was dark, there was a tapping at one of the living room windows, and a Santa Claus head appeared outside the dusky pane.

"It's Santa!" screamed Patrick, and ran outside, and came back in lugging a wastebasket containing Ethel and a box of ginger snaps. The duck had a red bow tied around its neck.

Patrick declared his loud intention of allowing Ethel to sleep in the bedroom he shared with Danny. Ethel could sleep in the wastebasket, he said. He would cut up some paper and make Ethel a nest, he said. Expecting Danny's protest, he put fingers in his ears.

Danny didn't protest. In his bathrobe, he followed Lily to the kitchen and watched as she measured sugar and water for the Christmas taffy. "Mama's never turned out right," he said. "She always cooked it too much or not enough. She always put too much vinegar in it."

"Mine is going to be spectacular," said Lily. "You can help me pull it when it's ready if you want to. Right now you can butter the pans for me if you feel like it."

Danny buttered two pans, washed his hands at the sink, and sat at the table. "I wonder where Mama is now."

Lily spoke what she had come to believe. "We don't need to know about that. All we need to know about is where we are. You and Patrick and Papa and me."

Danny pretended to yawn. He pretended a great interest in his bathrobe buttons. And softly then, speaking softly and calmly, opened the door to the place where he had lived alone for so long. "Waite Cody wasn't the first one with her," he said. "There was another one. It was when we lived in Wyoming. She said he was selling vacuum cleaners, but he didn't have any. Not even one. I was sick that day, and my teacher sent me home early."

The kitchen was so still, so still. The clock on its shelf above the sink ticked away a full half minute before Lily found her voice. "Did you tell Papa, Danny?"

"No," said Danny. "I never told anybody up till now."

"Then we mustn't tell him," said Lily, sure of yet another belief: That if he were told he wouldn't believe. Or if he believed, it wouldn't change anything. After a while maybe he would stop listening for Martha's footstep on the night porch, would be able to relax in the evenings instead of jumping at the sound of every passing car. Maybe after a while his eyes would lose their scorched look and he would laugh again.

Lily was positive that the house in the hollow would make a difference. She had wanted it to be her Christmas present to her family, but it was February before it and its furniture were finished and ready to give.

Lily asked Doe to be at the house at ten o'clock that Sunday morning, but he stayed away. Tactfully, so did Silent Joe and the lionhearts.

On the way from Sweet Root to the Falls, Judson said, "I don't remember this road being so bumpy."

"It's not the road," said Lily. "It's the car. You don't drive it enough."

"I ought to be at the store," said Judson. "There are always a couple of Sunday customers."

"Don't think about customers," said Lily. "Think about us."

"This is no day for a picnic," grumbled Judson. "It's going to rain."

"It is not going to rain," said Lily. It didn't dare. But it did dare. The drizzle started just as Judson turned the car into the hollow. Today it had a northerly look. Some of the trees were bare.

Judson drove the car past the privy, stopped, and backed up. "That building out there," he said. "It's on our land. It doesn't belong there."

"It belongs there," said Lily. "I put it there. It's our privy."

Judson got out of the car and stood in the road gazing at the privy. The trees were dripping.

Lily got out of the car to stand beside her father. "It's to go with our house," she said. "The beds don't have mattresses yet, and the curtains for the windows aren't made yet, but let's go look at it."

What a day it was. Patrick and Danny tore around touching everything. "This is really our house?" they cried. "This is our furniture? Really?"

"Really," said Lily, and pretended not to see her father standing in the doorway. He was crying a little. She had laid wood for a fire but had forgotten matches.

Her father said it didn't matter, that they could imagine they had a fire. He was so excited he scarcely touched his part of the picnic lunch eaten from the bare table. He began to talk about peanut farming. "We'll keep the store until we can get going with it," he said.

"Papa," said Lily, "we don't know the first thing about growing peanuts."

"Child," glowed Judson, "I'm afraid you don't know your old Papa. I'm like this. When somebody asks me if I know how to do something and I want to do it but don't know how, I tell them I do. Then I run off and find out. And I'm not the only one in this family who does that. You do it, too, don't you?"

"Yes," admitted Lily. "I've noticed that recently I've been doing that."

Patrick threw his arms around Lily with such force that she was almost knocked from her chair. "Lily, we're going to have a peanut farm!"

On a long intake of breath, Lily said, "Yes." And then with a strengthening of vision said it again. "Yes, we're going to have a peanut farm." It can happen, she thought. We can make it happen. Papa can supervise, that will be his job. I'll let him drop a few seeds. The rest of us will do the hard work. I can learn how to handle a plow. And mules. Doe or Silent Joe will teach me. And I'll get Billy Bragg out here to help, too. He doesn't need to poke around that station of his till nine o'clock every night. Everything else in Sweet Root is closed by six. Billy can close up, too, and get out here and help us. We will be good for him. I'll be good for him. He needs to get to know somebody like me.